FORGOTTEN OATH

FORGOTTEN OATH

DOROTHEA N. BUCKINGHAM

atmosphere press

For Tyler, Sean, and TeVaka

CHAPTER ONE

We filed off the school bus looking like a prison work gang, all of us in our orange Waikiki Intermediate School T-shirts and our closed-toe shoes. T-shirts so we could be identified in case we escaped and closed-toe shoes because Miss Nainoa warned us that the cemetery was littered with broken glass.

Miss Nainoa waved her clipboard over her head. "Noah, Blaise, pick up the pace."

My cousin Blaise elbowed me in the ribs. "What's the rush? It's not like the dead guys are going anywhere."

Blaise at his wittiest best.

"Gather round class." Miss Nainoa, even standing on her tiptoes, was still shorter than most of our class. "Hurry. We've only got three hours to get our work done."

Three years couldn't put a dent in the place.

The Mission Houses Cemetery was a graveyard of toppled headstones, broken bottles, and cat-licked-clean food cans. One grave had a statue of an angel with a missing wing; another had a statue of a Scottie dog with a yellow spray-painted butt.

I nudged Blaise. "Do you think they were so rich they buried their dog with them?"

"They might have been rich, but no one's taking care of them now." Blaise shook his head. "Can you imagine if we let

Tutu's or Papa's grave look like this?"

Noah and Blaise had the same grandparents—Tutu Kekoa and Papa. Their daughters were Blaise's and Noah's moms.

"Tutu would come back to haunt us," Blaise said.

"I laughed. And tell us more stories."

"Listen up, class." And for the 500th time, Miss Nainoa told us how to clean a cemetery headstone. "Swirl your sponge gently and be respectful of the dead."

Frank Santos crept up behind us. "Be respectful of the dead," he mocked Miss Nainoa. "Dead people. Woo-hoo."

Blaise looked at me. "Yeah, spirits and family ghosts."

Frank raised his eyebrows. "Family ghosts?"

"The Kekoa family curse," Blaise told him.

"Knock it off, Blaise," I said.

Blaise hunched his shoulders and whispered, "The Kekoa family is cursed."

"You're not funny," I said.

Blaise grinned. "The Night Marchers are coming for one of us." He looked at me.

I shoved Blaise so hard he stumbled into Frank.

Miss Nainoa clapped her hands. "Settle down." She pointed to a rusted-out shed. "Make a line."

The shed was a corrugated tin-roofed hut.

"Pick up your duffle bags. Each bag has an index card tied to it with a plot number of the grave you'll be cleaning."

Miss Nainoa droned on, but I wasn't listening. I was watching a homeless guy walk toward a backyard fenced in by a low, lava rock wall and a wrought-iron gate. He was probably wondering what a busload of kids was doing in his cemetery.

He caught me looking at him and tipped his hat, and I waved to him like some kindergarten kid waving to his best friend from across the room.

He had on a wide-brimmed black hat and a black jacket buttoned to his collar—a great outfit for a 90-degree day! From what I could see of his face, between his hat and long shaggy hair, he looked harmless. Shaggy, that's it. It was a good name for him.

Blaise was still running his mouth about "the Kekoa family curse." He grabbed Frank's arm. "Frank, has Noah ever told you he's 'The Chosen One'?"

"Leave it alone, Blaise." I gave him a quit-it-or-I'm-going-to pummel-you look, which was pretty much worthless because we both knew I'd never do it and if I ever tried, Blaise would wipe the sidewalk with me.

He kept telling Frank the story. "When we were little, our Tutu Kekoa babysat us. Sometimes at night after dinner, she'd sit us down at the kitchen table and take our hands in hers. Then, she'd lean over and whisper, 'You boys should know your family history.'"

Miss Nainoa clapped her hands. "Class. There are coolers of water bottles under the table. Make sure you stay hydrated."

Blaise didn't stop while Miss Nainoa was talking. "Our Tutu talked to spirits," he said.

"Our Tutu was an old woman who told stories," I said.

"You know they were real," Blaise said.

"Right. Family curses. Night Marchers. And spirits that don't rest."

Blaise smirked. "One night, when our grandfather was deep in the valley, he heard the pounding of drums." Blaise made his voice warble like our grandmother's did. "Our Papa heard the chant of warriors! Then the wind blew, and the sky turned orange and fire flowed down the valley like lava. It was the Night Marchers!

"Papa knew it was forbidden to look into the face of a Night Marcher. He knew it was punishable by death. He should have lain face down on the ground. But whether by accident or too much courage, he looked at a Marcher straight in the eye, and the Night Marcher raised his spear, ready to strike.

"Papa begged for his life, 'Spare me. I'll do anything you ask.' The Night Marcher took pity on our Papa, and in exchange for sparing his life, he made Papa swear to save the life of someone in his family."

Miss Nainoa was walking straight at us. Her glare was aimed at Blaise. I should have warned him, but I didn't. I watched, knowing she could be as fierce as any imaginary Night Marcher.

Blaise kept blabbing, oblivious. "Our Tutu would reach for Noah's hand and—," Blaise stopped mid-sentence.

Busted!

Miss Nainoa stopped right in front of him. She crossed her arms and said, "Do you boys have something to talk about that I should know?"

"No, ma'am," we answered together.

"Then get to the shed and pick up your stuff."

By the time we walked over, we were the last three in line.

The shed was as much of a dump as the rest of the place: black swivel chairs, plaster-splattered Home Depot buckets, twisted folding chairs, and an empty chicken coop that was being ignored by the roaming chickens.

There were only three duffle bags left. One of them was a moldy hot mess.

Frank snatched one of the clean ones, and I reached in front of Blaise to claim the other one, but when I did, a gust of dirt whirled around me. It blinded me for a second, and I turned away, rubbing my eyes. When I opened them again, I saw Blaise holding the last clean duffle.

"Guess that one was meant for you." He pointed to the ratty one.

"That's fine." I picked it up, pretending I didn't care.

The three of us looked at our index cards.

Just my luck, Frank and Blaise got graves in the main part of the cemetery with all the other kids. I had a hand-drawn map on my card that showed my grave being in the small yard on the side of the church, away from everybody else.

"My guy's buried way over there." I showed them my map.

"Why do you think?" Frank asked.

Blaise said, "Maybe he was a murderer, and the missionaries wouldn't let him be buried with the good people."

"Or maybe they were so rich they had their own separate spot," I said.

"Yeah, rich people do that all the time," Frank agreed.

The problem was, I didn't believe it and I wasn't excited to be so far away from everyone else. I looked over at the yard. Sure, rich people. Ha, like Shaggy!

I watched Shaggy sit on the lava rock wall and toss pebbles into a shopping cart filled with junk. I hoisted my duffle bag over my shoulder and grabbed the last straw mat on the table.

I looked over at Shaggy again. I was sure he was harmless. After all, this was his place, and we were the intruders. But I still wasn't thrilled about being alone with him.

I was afraid Blaise would make fun of me, but I asked him and Frank anyway, "Do you think I should tell Miss Nainoa about the guy?"

"What guy?" Frank asked. "I don't see any guy."

I looked back. Shaggy was gone.

"See, Frank, I told you my cousin was cursed. He's seeing ghosts now."

"Whatever." I didn't care what he thought. I trudged through the mud and pushed open the iron gate.

When I did, the hinges squealed like one in a cheap horror movie.

CHAPTER TWO

Horror movie! I'm in a horror movie: Blaise blabbing to Frank about my grandmother's ghost stories. Check. Bad luck with a blinding gust of wind. Check. Getting banished to a creepy part of the cemetery. Check. And then there was Shaggy.

I was sure I'd never live to see my thirteenth birthday.

I tossed my duffle in front of the headstone. It looked more like a mound of weeds with a jagged stone head sticking out of it.

Shaggy was sitting on the lava wall, humming, then he stopped tossing pebbles; he moved on to dragging a twig through a puddle of mud.

I couldn't imagine living like that. No house. No bed. No refrigerator stocked with Costco cookies.

I crouched down, inhaled the perfume of stale pee and rotten food, and emptied my bag: three thin white trash bags, a small plastic bucket, a rusted spade, work gloves, a package of craft sticks.

What I really needed was a bulldozer.

I started with the trash: 7-Eleven cups, McDonald's bags, broken bottles, newspapers, and soggy cardboard.

After a while, both my trash bags were full, and my soaked orange T-shirt clung to me like an orange peel.

The main part of the cemetery was shaded by sprawling

monkeypod trees. The only tree in my part of the cemetery was a *hala*, and the only shadow it cast was from its roots that were stacked against its trunk like a pyramid of bones. Ha! A tree with roots that looked like a stack of dead bones. Perfect for a cemetery.

I was hot, lonely, and tired, and I glared at Blaise and Frank dousing their stones with water, then turning their hoses on each other.

Typical, Blaise talks a big game, but I'm always the one who ends up doing the dirty work.

I slammed half a bottle of water and poured the rest over my head, then went back to work. I pulled weeds out of the ground and tugged the roots off the headstone. After a while, I could make out a few letters, then finally I saw a name: "Lopaka Aiona."

Then words appeared:

La Hanau 1820.
La Pio 1834.

My Tutu used to come into my room every birthday morning and wake me up singing her own tune of *Hauʻoli Lā Hānau*. She was always off-key and loud.

Lā Hānau. I figured it had to mean birth date and *La Pio* meant death date.

I did the math: Lopaka was fourteen when he died.

How do you die at fourteen?

I wondered if Lopaka was an ocean voyager who drowned trying to save someone in a storm. Or maybe he was a warrior for King Kamehameha?

That was it! He was a warrior ready for battle!

I imagined him marching up Nuʻuanu Pali, wearing a *tapa malo* and a pierced gourd helmet. He was leading the other warriors, fierce, bold, holding his spear over his head. The feet of the warriors pounded the ground, and the air trembled with the sound of their chanting.

A war chant! A *ha'a*. But the only one I knew was the university's football chant. I sang it loud:

`Mokomoko*. Fighting stance.

I held my chisel high.

Kaena Pa. Boast, begin!

I struck the stone!

Eia makou na puali koa o Hawai'i. Here we are, fearless warriors of Hawai'i

I pounded the chisel to the rhythm of the chant.

E ku mehe Ku, e Ku! E Ku! Stand as Ku, spirit of manhood. Stand! Stand!

E Ku!

I struck the stone.

E Ku lanakila! Oh, Ku, spirit of victory.

E Kui nui a kea! Oh, Ku, spirit of the vastly powerful.

Sparks flew off the stone!

E Ku I ke koa o Hawai'i e. Stand to the courage of all Hawai'i.

Then a chip of the headstone flew out . . . and I wasn't a warrior anymore! I was a sixth-grade kid who broke a two-hundred-year-old headstone.

I looked back to see if Miss Nainoa caught me, but she was in the main cemetery, scolding Blaise and Frank for fooling around.

OK, she didn't see me, and I knew Lopaka wouldn't care if I struck a chip off his old block. Ha, "chip off the old block!" Sometimes, even I thought my jokes were lame.

Out of the corner of my eye, I saw Shaggy staring at me.

Ignore him, I thought. Just find the chip and put it back. I raked my hands through the weeds, but I didn't find it. When I hit a patch of sleeping grass, I decided to give up. Slicing up my fingers wasn't worth the trouble. Besides, what difference would it make if I found it anyway? I probably couldn't stick it back in.

When I turned back to the grave, I spied a leather pouch

on the ground. I picked it out of the weeds and brushed it off. It was the color of sand and as soft as the chamois cloth my dad used to wash his truck. It had a few scuffs and some grass stains, and the leather cord was flaking, but as soon as I picked it up, I knew I had to keep it.

"Leave it be!" Shaggy yelled.

What was his problem? It wasn't like I was stealing from the dead—or the living either. The kid who lost it would never find it again.

I looked it over. It was the perfect size to keep Papa's old cat's eye marbles. The marbles were the last things he ever gave me.

Shaggy stood up and started walking toward me. "It's not yours!" he shouted.

I held my hands up in surrender. "OK! OK!" I tossed the pouch on the ground, and Shaggy backed off. He walked back to the wall, picked up the twig, and went back to swirling mud. By that time, my heart had slowed down to almost normal.

Then Shaggy said, "Smart boy. Just leave it be," and my heart started pounding again.

When Shaggy looked up, I glanced at his eyes—gray, dead shark eyes. "It's of no concern of yours, boy," he said.

Shaggy spoke with an accent. Maybe British? I wondered how a British guy ended up homeless in Hawaii.

I went back to working on Lopaka's grave, rubbing and scraping and thinking about the pouch.

I looked down and memorized where the pouch was on the ground, about two feet to the right of Lopaka's stone and a foot to the left of the *hala* tree. It would be easy to find. I knew Shaggy wouldn't be there forever. I was already planning to bike through the cemetery on my way home to get it.

Papa would have been so proud of me, finding a treasure in the middle of rubbish. I remembered the day he gave me his marbles. He was sitting in the carport on a broken-down chair that he found in the dump. He reached deep in his pocket and opened his hand to show me his marble collection.

I missed hanging out with Papa. I missed him playing cards with me, I missed him taking me to the dump. I remembered how he'd tell Tutu he was taking me out for an ice cream, and if he winked at me when he said it, I knew we were going to the dump.

But back to work. The quicker I finished, the quicker I was out of there.

My next step was to wash the stone, but the water spigot was on the other side of the yard, past Shaggy, in a far corner.

I walked as close to the opposite wall, as far away from Shaggy as I could, keeping my eyes down. But I accidentally looked at him, at his gray shark eyes.

I turned on the spigot and filled my bucket. The whole time I felt him staring at me, and when I walked back to Lopaka's grave, I kept my eyes glued to the ground.

I set the bucket down, dipped my sponge in the water, and swirled it over the stone, hearing Miss Nainoa's words in my head: "Swirl your sponge gently. Be respectful of the dead."

Then I heard a voice say, "Help him! You promised!"

I looked over at Shaggy. It wasn't him; he was still playing in the mud. Besides, the voice didn't have a British accent.

OK, I thought, it must have been the wind.

Then I heard it again: "Help him!"

That's it. I'm out of here! I tossed my sponge in the bucket and hightailed it out of there. I swung open the gate and crashed right into Miss Nainoa.

"Noah!" She caught me from falling. "What are you doing out here?"

I nodded, panting. "Cleaning a grave."

"There shouldn't be any grave out there." Miss Nainoa leafed through the papers on her clipboard. "What's the plot number?"

"My card was more like a map," I said.

"Let's see that map." She barreled through the gate, tucking her clipboard under her arm and slinging her water bottle over her shoulder.

I followed her, walking slowly, hoping the voice wouldn't come back, then hoping it would because if Miss Nainoa heard it, then I knew I wasn't crazy.

She put her water bottle down in front of Lopaka's stone, and I showed her my card, and she looked around, matching the tree and the wall with the map.

"Is this the only grave here?" she asked.

"Yes, miss."

She leaned over and ran her fingers over the letters of Lopaka's name. "I wonder why he's buried out here?"

"Blaise thinks Lopaka might be a murderer, and the missionaries didn't want him buried with the good people."

"Oh, does he?" She lowered her sunglasses and raised her eyebrows. "And is Blaise a cemetery historian?"

"No, miss."

She leaned in closer and read, "Lopaka Aiona, Lā Hānau 1820. *La Pio* 1834. That's strange." She stood up and pulled out her phone. "It usually says *La make* for the death date." Then she thumbed a few words into her phone and read, "*Pio*. It means 'captured' or 'disappeared like a ship at sea' or 'to go out of sight.'" She slid her phone back into her jeans. "I think I remember the *kupuna* saying it, but they said it like it was a sinking hope." She turned to me. "Strange."

She didn't have a clue how strange it was.

She ran her finger over the words again and a chip fell off.

Great, I thought, it wasn't just me.

She shook her head. "Every stone in this place is crumbling." She picked up the craft stick. "Let's see what we can do." She slid the stick down the *L* in Lopaka's name. "You've got to be gentle, especially when you dig this stuff out." She flicked a dead roach out of the letter and handed the stick back to me. "Now, you do it."

13

As I dragged the depressor down the K, Miss Nainoa whispered, "Use slow, gentle pressure."

When I was done, she said, "*Maika'i.*" Good job. "Finish up that letter and pack up your stuff. I'll let the director know we didn't finish." She looked over to where Shaggy was; she had to have seen him.

"I don't like you out here alone." She picked up her clipboard. "Clean up what you're doing and meet me in the shed."

And as soon as she turned the corner of the church, I threw all my stuff in the duffle. I figured I cleaned up enough!

I hoisted the bag over my shoulder and looked at Lopaka's grave, at Shaggy, at the *hala* tree. It all looked so ordinary.

By the time I got to the shed, Miss Nainoa was standing on an old wood crate. "Listen up, class." She waited a few seconds, then repeated, "Listen up. The Historical Society director offered to give us a tour of the old mission church. This is a very special treat," she said. "Stop what you're doing and meet at the top of the church steps."

Blaise, Frank, and I were standing at the church steps when Miss Nainoa summoned me with the curl of her finger. "Noah, I left my water bottle at your grave. Would you mind getting it for me?"

First of all, it wasn't "my" grave, and, second, I did mind.

I elbowed Blaise and said, "Let's go, cuz."

Miss Nainoa raised her hand. "Noah, I think you're capable of picking up a water bottle by yourself."

It wasn't the water bottle that I was worried about.

I shuffled toward the yard, scraping my feet loudly to scare away anyone or anything that was asking me for help.

Just grab the bottle and get out of there. I repeated it over and over: There are no such things as ghosts. No such thing as wandering spirits or the Kekoa curse. Just grab the bottle and go.

The closer I got, the faster I repeated it.

I opened the gate. Shaggy was gone! That was one worry down.

I forced my feet to keep walking.

The water bottle was just where Miss Nainoa left it, leaning against the headstone. Holding my breath, I picked it up. Nothing happened. No voice. No wind. No Shaggy.

That wasn't hard! And I convinced myself the voice must have been the wind. Now, head back to the church, I ordered myself.

That's when I spotted the pouch. Every cell in my body told me to forget it. Keep walking. Let the whole cemetery thing go, and get back with the rest of the class. But I couldn't.

The pouch was right there, and it was meant for me.

I bent down, picked it up, and put the string around my neck. As soon as I did, I was somewhere else.

I was standing in an old fishing village with my wrists tied with a rope.

CHAPTER THREE

"Keep walking!" A man wearing a rifle slung across his chest bumped into me.

Mud oozed through a leather boot I wore on one foot. On my other foot, I had a braided leaf boot.

"Stop gawking!" the man yelled.

He had an animal vest on and chaps like a cowboy.

Gawking? I was trying to figure out where I was.

A Hawaiian man was tied to me with the same rope that held my wrists. He was bare-chested with braided, black hair down to his waist. On his left shoulder was a shark tattoo.

He walked staring straight ahead. There were about twenty of us, all men, all in old-fashioned clothes.

I looked down at mine. The pouch dangled over a billowy white shirt and my jeans turned into button-fly black trousers.

Wherever I was, it had to be at least one hundred years ago. I saw a blacksmith's shop, a sailmaker's, a "provision" store, whatever that was, and in the distance, in the harbor, there were dozens of tall-masted ships. Maybe I was on Maui during whaling days? But there was a snow-capped mountain in the distance, so I had to be on the Big Island.

But was any of it real? Could I have fallen when I put the pouch on? Hit my head? Or did Shaggy clunk me with a rock? Whatever happened, I knew what I was seeing wasn't real.

I told myself to relax.

Think: You were on a school field trip. You're in downtown Honolulu. I shut my eyes tight. I knew Blaise would be right there next to me when I opened them. But I was still there.

Breathe. One, two, three. Breathe.

I told myself I was just imagining it. But the whole time I felt the rope cutting into my wrist.

I tugged on the rope. "Where are we?"

When he turned, I saw he wasn't a man but a boy about my age.

He said, "Reverend Newhouse's church is just ahead," as if I should know who Reverend Newhouse was.

"What's going on?"

"Hush." He stared straight ahead.

I checked out the other men. I figured they were all hunters because they all carried rifles or had knives tucked in their belts. At the front of the group, four men were carrying a six-foot canvas sling between two bamboo poles. Maybe they killed a pig? But I doubted we were going to a luau—not with me and this other kid tied up.

When we walked past people standing in front of the shops, they glared at me. One guy spit on the ground.

"What's happening?"

"Noah, we told you not to come back."

He knew my name.

"How do you know who I am?"

"What's wrong with you? Don't you remember anything? We told you not to come back."

"I've never been here before."

"Try to remember," he said.

"Who are you?" I asked.

"Lopaka."

"Lopaka Aiona?"

He nodded.

"What am I doing here?"

"I don't know. We told you to save yourself and never come back. You should have listened to us."

"Who is 'us'?"

"Me and your grandfather," he said. "Noah, have you forgotten everything?"

"Why am I here?"

"You promised to save me."

"No way," I said. "Just no. My name is Noah Kekoa Silva and I'm a seventh-grade kid on a school service project."

"Do you remember meeting a Night Marcher?"

I remember making fun of kids who believed in them.

"Once, when you were with your grandfather, you promised a Night Marcher you would save my life."

I didn't answer.

"Do you remember your dream?" he asked.

I used to have nightmares about Night Marchers and Papa, but I wasn't going to tell him that.

I answered, "No."

"Look at your hand. It has the mark of the Night Marcher."

"I've always had that. It's a birthmark," I said.

"Do you remember when we first met? We were in the mountains, and you showed it to me. You told me a Night Marcher marked you."

"Move it." A *haole* man, maybe three feet tall, jabbed me with his rifle. "Move!" The man's head came up to my chest. His torso was long, and his legs were short and bowed. Despite his height, his voice boomed like a cannon. "Go!" he ordered me.

Once the man walked ahead of us, Lopaka said, "Don't anger Little William. He's the only one who believes us."

I was swirling down a hole. Every word I heard, everything I saw was getting me into a worse place.

"Why are we tied up?" I asked Lopaka.

"We were captured."

The sound of the word "captured" felt like a lightning bolt in my gut. I remembered Miss Nainoa translating the word *pio* on Lopaka's grave. One of the meanings was "captured."

For sure, I was captured, but why? The last thing I remembered was putting on the pouch.

The pouch! That was it. I was sure that if I took it off, I'd be back home, but I couldn't lift my hands because the rope between Lopaka and me was so taut.

"Come closer," I told Lopaka.

"Why?"

"So, I can lift my arms and take off the pouch, then I'll go home."

He shook his head. "If you take it off, you'll be stuck in the past."

This was a no-win situation. Either Lopaka was telling the truth or he wanted to keep me in the past to save him. I had to figure out what was going on.

The farther up the hill we walked, the fewer shops there were and there were more open fields. And the more I walked, the foot with the ti leaf sandal throbbed.

If the Kekoa family curse was true, why wasn't Papa there? Then I caught myself thinking what was happening was real. No, I told myself, it's all a hallucination. You must have fallen or passed out or got dehydrated. None of this is happening.

We kept walking.

I thought of Blaise. He had to still be in the church, listening to the director's talk. I wished he knew I was in trouble. I knew he'd help me.

"We're almost there," Lopaka said.

There were clusters of thatched huts with bamboo fences around their yards where chickens and pigs roamed freely.

At the fork in the road, we made a left, and at the top of the hill was a white clapboard church, a house, an open-wall *hale* with a few men under its thatched roof.

When we got closer, I scanned the men to look for Papa.

I knew it made no sense to look for him, but it didn't matter; I was desperate for help. There were more hunters and a few *paniolo* in chaps and cowboy hats, but behind the church, near the chicken coop, I swore I saw an old man with gray popcorn hair wearing a red T-shirt just like Papa's. I squinted to get a clearer look, but the man disappeared.

My worlds were colliding. If Papa was there, was this all real?

The men in the *hale* made way for the men carrying the canvas bundle. When they did, I saw two tables—one was empty, the other had a canvas bundle on it about the same size as ours.

Four hunters helped the men set the bundle on the table, grunting as they hauled it.

I wanted to ask Lopaka what was in the canvas, but he was staring straight ahead.

At the edge of the crowd, Little William waved his arms. "Make room for the reverend." The men stepped back, clearing a path for the reverend.

He was a tall man. His beard was long and gray, and he walked with his head bent over as if he were ducking under a too-low door.

"Make way for Reverend Newhouse." Little William pushed back men twice his height.

Following the reverend out of his house was a small blonde girl carrying an egg basket as she walked toward the chicken coop. The girl stopped mid-stride and gawked at all of us.

The reverend turned to her. "Tend to your chores, Abagail."

"Yes, Father." She nodded and walked toward the coop.

None of the men spoke to Reverend Newhouse. A few whispered among themselves and pointed at Lopaka and me.

Little William grabbed the rope connecting me and Lopaka, led us inside, and told us to stand at the foot of the table. Looking at the bundle on the table, I was sure it was a pig—it was big and round and the canvas was stained with blood.

One man standing on the side of the table was wearing a silver-studded vest and a hat with a feather lei. He looked straight at me, then he ran his index finger across his neck.

CHAPTER FOUR

Reverend Newhouse waited for the men to quiet down, then said, "We are here to determine how our beloved Doctor Douglas died."

Was Douglas's body in the canvas? It looked too short to be a body. Maybe it was only part of his body?

Reverend Newhouse gestured to a bald man with wire-rimmed glasses and a lower lip that protruded far enough to cast a shadow. The reverend said, "We will do a complete examination. Mr. Wilcocks will take the measurements and Mr. Harrison will record the findings." Harrison was a muscular man who was poised with an open notebook and a pencil in his hand.

Reverend Newhouse continued. "Little William will bear witness to the proceedings."

Little William dragged a three-legged stool up to the table. When he stood on it, his head was level with the bundle.

I never saw a dead body before. When Papa and Tutu died, their bodies were cremated. There were urns at their funerals and photos of them draped with leis—but no bodies.

While the men were untying the sling, Reverend Newhouse walked around the table, stopping behind Lopaka. The reverend whispered something to Lopaka; Lopaka looked at the reverend and shook his head no.

Reverend Newhouse went back to the head of the table. "We are here to examine the body of Doctor David Douglas. We know his body was found in an open pit built to trap bulls on the property of Jack Finn. All else is conjecture."

The men untied the ropes around the canvas sling, and I closed my eyes. I heard the ropes drop to the ground and men murmur and felt the shove the them as they moved closer to the table. Then I heard Little William say, "This bull couldn't kill a fly."

I opened my eyes. It wasn't a body on the table; it was the head of a bull.

Men mumbled and nudged each other to get a closer look.

"Silence," the reverend ordered.

I looked at Lopaka and he jutted his chin toward the other table.

Was he trying to tell me that the other bundle had the body of Doctor Douglas?

Mr. Wilcocks measured the bull's horns. "The horns are two inches in height and visibly ground down."

The *paniolo* who ran his finger across his neck pushed his way to the front. He was standing so close to me that I could smell his breath. The cowboy leaned over and rubbed the bull's horns. "They're ground to the nubs."

Little William, who was directly across the table from him, smiled. "So, the great cowboy, Louis Sanchez, agrees with me! A bull didn't kill Doctor Douglas." Little William looked at the men around the table. "Let's see if he'll agree it was Jack Finn who did."

"It wasn't Finn! They killed him!" Sanchez turned toward me and shoved his finger into my chest. "Why else would they have the gold?"

That's why we were tied up; they thought we killed Douglas! So, that was it. I traveled to the past to save Lopaka from being accused of murder. But what about me? There was nothing in the curse about me needing to be saved.

"Finn's a good man." Sanchez turned back to Little William. "He's a good hunter and a good provider for his family."

Little William admitted, "Finn's the best hunter on the island. We all agree to that. And we all know he wields the power of being the governor's hunter. And I'll bet money that there's not a man here who hasn't been bullied or threatened or bribed by the 'good hunter,' Jack Finn." William went on sarcastically, "The 'good family provider.'"

Reverend asked, "Where is Mr. Finn?"

Mr. Harrison told Reverend Newhouse, "We hit a flash flood in the mountains, and Finn went back to his family to make sure they were safe."

"He'll be back in the morning," Sanchez said.

"Sure, he'll be back," William scoffed. "And he'll confess to murder and hang himself too."

Sanchez slammed the table. "Open your eyes, William! It was them who did it. They had Douglas's gold."

"No!" Reverend stared at Sanchez. "Those are all things we are here to consider." He waited for Sanchez to calm. "Mr. Sanchez, neither I nor anyone here is to assume Mr. Finn is innocent." Then he turned to Little William. "Neither should we assume he is guilty."

William challenged the reverend. "You think Finn's guilty too. You know the kind of man Finn is. Tell them."

Reverend Newhouse spoke calmly, "What disposition of personality Mr. Finn has is none of our concern."

Little William and Harrison exchanged glances, and from the way they looked at each other, I believed they both thought Finn was guilty.

Reverend Newhouse addressed Mr. Wilcocks, "We shall continue," and Mr. Wilcocks concluded the measurements.

When the measurements were completed and recorded and the bull's head was re-wrapped, Reverend Newhouse said, "Now we shall examine the body of Doctor Douglas." And we all moved to the other table.

When they unwrapped the canvas, there was the body!

Mr. Wilcocks began, "Here lies the body of Doctor David Douglas. Approximate height, five feet, four inches. Approximate weight, 130 pounds."

Mr. Harrison lifted the body by its armpits, and Mr. Wilcocks removed Douglas's jacket and shirt. I tried not to look at the doctor's face.

They set the body back down. The doctor's arms were caught under him, propping his chest up. It was a hairy chest, matted with blood.

Mr. Wilcocks took a pair of calipers out of a toolbox. Then he ran his finger over the doctor's face. That was the first time I looked at Douglas. His eyes were open, and I swore he was staring right at me.

Mr. Wilcocks announced, "There are four gashes to the head. One over his left eye. A deep one behind his right ear. Another on his left temple and one on his right cheek."

Mr. Harrison recorded the measurements, then Mr. Wilcocks shuffled his way down the

As he tugged out Douglas's arm, the hunters leaned in closer. And when Mr. Wilcocks held up the arm, these hunters, whose job it was to kill and slaughter bulls, gasped.

CHAPTER FIVE

Mr. Wilcocks held up the doctor's bloodied hand. "The fourth finger on the doctor's hand has been severed."

All that was left of it was a red, curdled stump.

Sanchez turned toward me. "As if murder wasn't enough for you two," Sanchez shouted.

Mr. Wilcocks continued his observation in a calm, methodical voice, "It is a clean cut, implying it was made by a knife."

"Of course, it was made by a knife. Finn's knife!" Little William challenged Sanchez, and Sanchez turned toward me. "It was them, I tell you." We were pushed together by the crowd.

"But neither of them had a knife," William protested.

"They tossed it," Sanchez insisted.

"No." Little William shook his head.

"They could have tossed it!" Sanchez shouted. "These two had the gold. They stole it, then they cut off the finger for the ring."

"But they didn't have a ring on them." William turned to the hunters as if he were presenting a case to a jury. "So, where is the ring?"

Sanchez shot his hand around my neck. "He's the murderer." He shoved my face into the doctor's body.

I couldn't breathe. I panicked and kicked and landed a blow in Sanchez's groin.

Sanchez buckled to the ground, two hunters grabbed me, and a third punched me in the gut. I collapsed on the ground, holding my belly.

"Stop!" Reverend Newhouse pushed aside the men and stood between me and Sanchez.

As he spoke, a skinny, red-haired boy helped me up, and the hunters helped Sanchez hobble to his feet.

Reverend Newhouse scanned the faces of all the men there. "Go home. All of you. Go home. Tend to your families and let me tend to this."

"What about those two?" Sanchez pointed to Lopaka and me.

"I'll keep them under watch," Reverend Newhouse assured.

"Tied up and guarded?" Sanchez challenged him.

"I give you my word, Mr. Sanchez. They will be well guarded."

Sanchez warned, "It's on your head if they escape, Reverend, and it will be you who will answer to the governor." Then he led the paniolo away, leaving only Reverend Newhouse, Mr. Wilcocks, Mr. Harrison, Lopaka, Jeremiah, and me.

"Are you OK, son?" Jeremiah asked me.

Son? This skinny kid with a red haze of a mustache and ears as big as his fists called me "son." Then he walked to Lopaka's side of the table and the two of them talked in whispers and glanced at me.

I didn't know who I could trust. Was Jeremiah a friend of Lopaka?

As Mr. Wilcocks finished up his examination, Reverend Newhouse asked Jeremiah if he could have the doctor's body ready to be transported by that night.

"Transported? Not buried?" Jeremiah asked.

"It's best if I send the body to Oahu. The doctors in Honolulu can decide how Douglas died."

"I'll need help," Jeremiah said. "We have coffins at the mill, but I need help with the body."

Reverend Newhouse turned to Lopaka. "Can you vouch

for this boy?" Newhouse asked.

"I can."

It seemed like everyone trusted Lopaka, but I was the one who was supposed to save him.

"Good." Reverend Newhouse nodded.

The reverend took Lopaka at his word. He was letting us loose! I thought that once the two of us got to the mill, we could escape.

Reverend Newhouse walked back to the parsonage where the girl who carried the egg basket was staring out the window.

The three of us loaded Douglas's body onto a wooden cart. We pushed the cart down the path; with every step, my foot throbbed. I was obviously hurt, but I didn't know how it happened.

As we made it down the hill, the mud got deeper, and it was harder to push the cart, but we kept going, putting our shoulders to it until it got stuck.

"We've got to lift it," Jeremiah said.

"Roll up your pants legs," Lopaka told me, and when he rolled his up, I saw a shark tooth tattoo on his right leg that matched the one on his left shoulder.

"On the count of three," Jeremiah called out. "Lift!"

When we got to the mill, we rolled the cart up a ramp and set it down next to a makeshift table made of narrow planks and sawhorses.

Then Jeremiah pulled Lopaka aside, and again, they whispered to each other. Then Jeremiah announced he was going down to the harbor to talk to his father. When I asked him if he was going to talk about us, Jeremiah shook his head and left.

Lopaka walked around the mill, eyeing the wall to the right of us and a long table with clamps attached to it. Above the table were rows of shelves bowed from the weight of planers, hand drills, clamps, and small saws curved like scythes. On the opposite wall, there were rows of lumber stacked higher than I ever saw at Lowe's or The Home Depot.

Lopaka moved around some jugs on the shelves. There were glasses jammed with paintbrushes and strips of linen with giant sewing needles pinned to them.

"Is there something you want me to do?" I asked.

"I can't find the twine." He pointed to a smaller table next to Douglas's body. "Could you check?"

Everything on the table was coated with sawdust. Even the air was filled with it.

I checked the top drawer. "Got it." I held up the twine.

Lopaka lined up the jars and tools that he got from the shelf. He opened the bottom drawer of the table and pulled out a rolled-up canvas.

"Is there anything else I can get?"

Lopaka slowly unrolled the canvas to expose several knives and chisels.

"My mallet. It's next to the bucket."

I watched him systematically set out all his tools. "How do you know what to do?"

"Jeremiah's father taught me."

"Do you work for him?"

He unwrapped Douglas's body from the bundle. "I never worked for him. After my parents died, Jeremiah's family took me in until we found my aunt."

"Your aunt?"

"Kia Manu. You saw her on the ridge."

I must have looked puzzled.

"The bird catcher. She collects feathers," he repeated.

I didn't remember being with Lopaka, but I wasn't going to say it again. Instead, I asked, "What does she do with the feathers?"

"She sews them into capes." Lopaka dipped a knife in the jar, then wiped it. "Her feathers are so perfect; they're made into the king's capes."

I saw lots of yellow-and-red feather capes during a field trip to the Bishop Museum. The guide told us it took thousands of feathers to sew together a long cape.

"When I was a boy, she'd take me on hunts with her," Lopaka said. "That's why I'm such a good guide."

I couldn't imagine Lopaka ever being a "boy." He acted more like a man than a kid.

"Sometimes she'd go out for months at a time," he said. "That's where she was when my parents died, so Jeremiah's family took me in until we could find her."

"Do you live with her now?"

He looked insulted. "I take care of myself. Kia Manu lives in a cave close to Jack Finn's ranch." He went back to working on Douglas's body. He straightened the doctor's legs and laid the doctor's arms down close to his ribs.

Lopaka asked me to get sea sponges from the shelf. I stared outside, thinking all I had to do was walk out and I'd be free—but to where?

I came back with the sponges, and Lopaka set a calabash of water next to Douglas's head.

"Now we clean his chest," Lopaka said. He dipped a sponge in the water and swirled it across the doctor's chest. "You do it," he said. "Use gentle pressure."

When he told me that, I heard Miss Nainoa's words in my head, "Use gentle pressure," but this time I was cleaning a dead body, not a gravestone.

We worked quietly. I was hoping that once Lopaka and I were alone, he'd tell me what he and Jeremiah whispered about, but he didn't.

I figured I had nothing to lose, so I asked, "Right before Jeremiah left for the harbor, what were you two talking about?"

He either didn't hear me or he was ignoring me.

I asked him again. "What did Jeremiah say to you right before he left?"

Lopaka picked up a knife. "You may want to sit over there."

He motioned to a stool next to a few cats that were curled in the sun.

"I don't need to," I said. I wanted to stay right with him and keep asking what was going to happen to us.

"I have to open the doctor," Lopaka said and cut a deep V from the top of Douglas's chest to his belly.

My eyes bulged. I felt my breakfast shoot up to my mouth, but I swallowed it back down.

Lopaka made two more cuts on Douglas's chest: one from the bottom of each shoulder to meet the one at the top of Douglas's chest so that it made a Y.

It was like autopsies on TV, but I was right there, watching the cuts being made. There was no blood, just long deep cuts.

"I need to keep the flaps open," Lopaka said. He lifted the skin away from Douglas's ribs and asked me to pin it back with a needle.

I ran a pin through the flap that held Douglas's chest open and I saw shimmering red and gray things that looked like lungs.

Lopaka held the other side back, and I pinned it too. Then he reached into Douglas's chest and pulled out what looked like his heart and tossed it in the bucket. When he tossed it, the cats frenzied, fighting over Douglas's guts. Then they carried them away.

The more Lopaka tossed, the more the cats came back, their whiskers red with blood.

When he was done, Douglas's chest was empty, and he said the next step was to "pack the body."

He pointed to the open wall. "The salt bin is outside on the right."

I walked out, looking toward the mountains, wondering if Papa was on the island. If I escaped, maybe I could find him. But where would I look?

I used a metal scoop to fill the bucket with salt. When the salt hit the welts on my wrists, it was instant pain. I brushed the salt off, but that only ground it deeper into my cuts.

I rolled down my sleeves to cover my wrists, but they weren't long enough. So, I took a deep breath, told myself I could do this, picked up the bucket, and brought it back to Lopaka.

He pointed to the empty space where Douglas's guts were and told me to pour the salt into it.

"I need at least two more buckets," he said.

I showed him my wrists. "The salt really burns."

His answer was, "There are gloves in the drawer." He acted like I was complaining. He should have been making things easy for me. I was there to save him! But right then, I didn't care if he got saved. I didn't trust him.

Putting on the leather gloves only made things worse, trapping the tiny pieces of salt in my skin, but I brought in the second bucket, and Lopaka asked for the third. By the third bucket, the stinging pain was just one more thing I was dealing with.

The last bucket filled Douglas's chest, then we hunched over Douglas's body. I squeezed the flaps tight, and Lopaka sewed them back together.

It took two of us to close Douglas's chest.

I was relieved to be over that, then Lopaka said, "I need three or four more buckets to fill the coffin with salt."

CHAPTER SIX

Lopaka spread a layer of salt in the coffin, then we laid Douglas's body on top of it. While we were shoving the doctor's arms into the coffin, Jeremiah ran into the sawmill.

He was panting, resting his hands on his knees. "It's not good news," he said. "Sanchez is going to Kohala to get the governor."

Lopaka didn't say anything.

Jeremiah said, "We've got to get you out of here."

"What's going on?" I asked.

Lopaka told me, "If the governor comes to Hilo to try our case, we'll both hang."

Jeremiah explained, "Jack Finn hunts bulls and sells them to the governor. Then, the governor sells the bull meat to ships' captains and makes a fortune."

"I saw lots of hunters here today. Why can't he buy meat from them?"

"Finn's the best," Jeremiah answered.

"And the other hunters are afraid to cross him," Lopaka said.

Jeremiah turned to Lopaka. "What do we do now that are plan won't work?"

They did have a plan. And it probably didn't include me.

"What was your plan?"

Jeremiah said that his father was trying to get the trial to be held on Oahu. "The governor there doesn't know Finn and the Honolulu doctors wouldn't be influenced by Sanchez. A trial here, with Kuakini as judge, will find you both guilty no matter what the truth is."

Lopaka said, "My only chance is for Kia Manu to get me to a sanctuary."

"What about me?" I asked.

"Maybe my father could get you signed on to a ship. You must have skills."

"What do you mean?"

"Skills," Lopaka repeated. "Can you read and write?"

"Of course."

"Can you do figures?" Jeremiah asked. "If you can keep ledgers and inventory, the whaling ships are always looking for crew." I couldn't believe I was planning to sign on to a whaling ship. There had to be a way to get back home.

After Jeremiah left to go back to the harbor, I asked Lopaka, "What about this thing?" I held up the leather pouch. "Can you get it to work to send me home?"

"Noah, I didn't send for you. Your grandfather did."

"If my grandfather had any sense of *kuleana*. Look around. I don't see my grandfather. Do you?"

"It's his *kuleana*," Lopaka insisted.

"Do you, or don't you have the power to send me home?" I asked Lopaka. "Answer me."

"Noah, your grandfather—"

"Stop talking about my grandfather!"

"You know your promise says if you don't save me, you'll die the same day I do."

"So, how can I save you?"

He didn't answer.

Think! But every idea I thought about wouldn't work. Then, I got it!

"What if I could find proof that you didn't kill Douglas

that was so strong, even Kuakini had to admit it was true?"

"What kind of proof?"

"Eyewitness accounts. A confession. Police reports." I talked fast. "In my time, I can read newspapers that were written hundreds of years before I was born. Maybe I could find evidence that won't be discovered until years from now? Maybe there was another witness? Maybe Finn will confess on his deathbed?" I talked faster, hoping to convince Lopaka to send me home.

"Can't you do it from here?" Lopaka asked.

"No. Only in my time."

"Noah, how do I know you'll come back?"

I told him I would, knowing full well I never intended to return.

"All right," Lopaka agreed. "Go home."

The next thing I knew, I was sitting on the ground near Lopaka's gravestone. A plane flew overhead. A police siren wailed, and a car's radio blasted.

I was home.

A mosquito landed on my arm, and I swatted it, smearing its blood. The mosquito was real. The blood was real, but so were the welts around my wrists from where ropes were tied to me in the past.

I yanked the pouch off my neck and flung it as far as I could.

"Noah!" It was Blaise. "Miss Nainoa sent me to look for you. Where've you been?"

If I told him, he'd never believe me.

"She probably thought you were kidnapped. Can you see it on the five o'clock news?" He lowered his voice and held his hand to his mouth like he was holding a microphone. "Waikiki Elementary student kidnapped from the Mission Houses Cemetery. Details after the break."

In a way, I was kidnapped.

"The director of the historical society told fourteen missionary stories so far. Fourteen! Frank counted. And every one of them was B-O-R-I-N-G. Boring. You're lucky you missed them."

Not that lucky, I thought.

"Wait until you get a look at him. Mr. Goodall, the director. Shaved head, beard, and *puka* jeans."

"And he's got a Harley Davidson belt buckle."

I staggered my first few steps.

"You OK?" Blaise asked.

"Yeah." I remembered I was there to get Miss Nainoa's water bottle.

"The only good story he told was about this famous ghost that haunts the cemetery."

I picked up the bottle, and we walked to the church together; as we did, Blaise filled me in on every detail. "The ghost steals stuff from visitors."

Blaise opened the door to the church; Miss Nainoa was right inside. She stopped me with a wag of her finger. "We'll talk about where you were later."

"Yes, miss." I handed her her water bottle and caught up with the rest of the class jammed under the choir staircase.

Mr. Goodall looked just like Blaise described. Shaved head, a Harley Davidson belt buckle, and a long beard knotted into a tassel.

Mr. Goodall stood in front of a headstone that was bolted to the wall. "Does anyone know who David Douglas was?"

Did he mean Doctor Douglas?

"Think about Douglas fir Christmas trees," Mr. Goodall said.

"They go for two hundred bucks for a nine-footer at Safeway," Frank said—his father was the manager of the Kapahulu Safeway.

"He was a botanist who lived in the 1800s and the tree is named after him. Douglas traveled the world discovering new plants and brought them back to England to be studied. He hiked thousands of miles all over the mainland and Canada and Hawai'i. In fact, he came to the islands three times.

"Sadly, during his last trip, he died on a hike from Kona to Hilo. He fell into a pit dug to trap bulls. Unfortunately, there was a live bull in it, and he was gored to death."

It was the same Douglas!

"A minister sent Douglas's body to Honolulu, so the British could send it home."

That's not why Reverend Newhouse sent it to Oahu.

"While they waited for a ship to send his body back to England, the missionaries temporarily buried him in our cemetery. But unfortunately, by the time the news got to London and a British navy officer came back to get it, years passed, and no one at the mission remembered where he was buried."

"You lost his body?" Frank asked.

"Not me personally." Mr. Goodall smiled. "Back then, it took years for letters to go back and forth between Honolulu and London. Finally, after the British decided that rather than shipping Douglas's body home, he should remain in Honolulu, they sent a headstone for his grave. But, like I said, unfortunately, no one knew where it was."

"That's a lot of unfortunately," Blaise whispered.

Mr. Goodall went on, "So when the headstone arrived, the pastor put it here. It's been here ever since."

Mr. Goodall faced the wall behind him where the headstone was bolted. He read it: "Here lies David Douglas. Born Scotland, 1799, Died Hawaii, May 30, 1834."

Frank raised his hand. "If Douglas was such a great hiker, how did he fall into a pit with a live bull in it? He had to see it."

"Or hear it," Blaise said. "The bull must have been moaning."

Miss Nainoa jumped in. "I appreciate your enthusiasm, but please don't interrupt the director while he's talking." It was amazing the way she could talk through her clenched teeth.

"Actually, I love the questions," Mr. Goodall said. "A lot of people wondered the same thing back then. Some people thought his guide killed him for his gold. His name was

Lopaka Aiona. We think Aiona is buried here, but we're not sure."

"Did you lose Lopaka's body too?" Frank asked.

"A few months after Douglas's death, a decomposed body of a boy about Lopaka's age was found in a cave near the bull pit. In those days, there wasn't DNA testing. They assumed it was Lopaka, but we can't be sure. So, we think he's buried in the back cemetery, but we're not sure."

"Was Aiona's body buried all alone because people thought he killed Douglas?" I asked.

"Noah, that's enough," Miss Nainoa said. "Mr. Goodall has other things to tell us."

"Actually, I'd like to answer that," he said. "I didn't quite hear your name. Is it Noah?"

"Yes."

"Noah, the story I heard is that when the body was found, the pastor on the Big Island wanted to bury it in the church cemetery there, but Governor Kuakini forbade it, saying Lopaka was a murderer. So, the pastor had the body shipped to Honolulu. But who knows what's true?"

"But do you think he killed Douglas?"

"No one knows for sure," Mr. Goodall said. "We've had historians from all over the world come here to do research.

"We have Douglas's journal in our cemetery archive. If you can call it an archive." He laughed. "It's more of a basement with memories, but if you're interested in the case, I could arrange for you to take a look through it."

Miss Nainoa said, "Noah, it could be an extra-credit project for you."

"No, thanks." I shook my head.

"Who knows?" Mr. Goodall said. "You may be the guy who solves the mystery."

CHAPTER SEVEN

After school, Blaise and I were biking home. When the light on Pohukaina

Street turned green, I said, "Follow me."

"Where to?"

"Just do it." I swerved right onto Punchbowl Street.

When we caught the next red light, Blaise asked, "Where are you taking me?"

"You'll see." And I led him down three more blocks, straight into the driveway of the Mission Houses Cemetery.

"Cuz, you gotta be kidding me." Blaise got off his bike.

"Before you say anything, listen to me. I'm going to tell you something, but you can't laugh. OK?"

"OK."

"And you got to believe me."

"OK. OK."

"And you can't tell anybody."

"Spit it out!"

"OK." I took a deep breath. "I have to show you something." As we walked to Lopaka's grave, I told him the whole story.

"Good one, cuz! You got me." Blaise punched me in the shoulder. "That's a better story than I could make up."

"I'm not kidding."

"You traveled back in time? You met a dead guy and he told you the Kekoa family curse was real?" He laughed so hard he coughed.

I showed him the welts on my wrist. "They're from where I was tied up."

He ran his finger over them.

"That hurts!" I snatched my hand back.

Blaise stared at my wrists. "The Kekoa curse is true? The whole Night Marcher story?"

I nodded.

"Did you see the Night Marchers?"

I shook my head.

"Was Papa there?"

"I don't know. I saw a guy with gray hair wearing a red T-shirt, but he disappeared."

"You saw a guy in a T-shirt hundreds of years ago and you wondered if it was Papa? He never took that shirt off."

"I'm not sure. It could have been a sailor's shirt. I didn't get a look at the guy's face. The whole thing was weird."

"How does it happen? Do you go through a time tunnel?"

"Nothing like that."

"So, how?"

"There's a pouch. I put it around my neck and I'm gone."

"Let's see it."

"I tossed it."

"Why?!"

"Because I'm never going back."

"You said the curse is true."

I nodded.

"That means you're leaving Papa's spirit never to rest?"

"Tutu didn't always say Papa's spirit wouldn't rest. Who knows? Maybe the guy I saw was Papa, maybe he wasn't. But whoever he was, he didn't help me."

"Maybe you didn't give him a chance!"

"You got to believe me!"

Blaise stared at the welts on my wrist. "I believe you," he said, "but it's hard." Blaise read the date on Lopaka's tomb. May 30. "But she always said the chosen one will die on the same day as the guy he's supposed to save, and that's in two days."

"Lopaka died over 200 years ago, and I'm still here!"

"Where's the pouch?" Blaise asked.

"I told you, I tossed it."

"Where?"

"I don't remember."

"You remember! Where is it?"

"Over there somewhere."

Blaise walked up and down, scraping his shoe through the grass. "Found it!" He held up the pouch. "How does it work?"

"You don't want to go back there!" I grabbed for it, but Blaise held it over his head. "You don't know what it's like."

"Do I say special words?" Then he put the pouch on! But nothing happened.

"Do I ask Papa for permission?" he asked me.

I shook my head.

"I'm here, Papa."

But nothing happened.

Blaise glared at me. "Liar!" He took the pouch off. "This isn't how you go back."

"It is too."

"The whole thing is a lie. You didn't travel to the past."

"I did."

Blaise shoved the pouch into my chest. "Then show me how you do it!"

"I'm not going back!"

"If there really is time travel, then you need to save Papa."

"I can't."

"Coward!"

"I'm not a coward!" I put the pouch around my neck and the next thing I knew I was back in the past, crouched behind a boulder with Lopaka right next to me.

CHAPTER EIGHT

Lopaka lunged at me! He pinned my forearms against the rock. "Who are you?"

"You know me. I'm Noah."

"I've never seen you," he said.

"I'm Noah Kekoa. Look at my hand!" I opened it wide. "It's a Night Marcher's mark."

He loosened his grip.

"A Night Marcher sent me to save you from being hanged."

"Hanged? For what?" Lopaka still held my arms down.

"For killing Doctor Douglas."

Lopaka scoffed. "The doctor's at camp."

"I'm telling you, he's going to get murdered, and people will think you did it."

"Why would they think that?" Lopaka asked.

"Because you had his gold when they captured you."

Lopaka let go of me and stepped back. He clutched a pouch tied to his waist. "The doctor gave me his gold for safekeeping," he said.

"But when the hunters capture you, they'll find you with Douglas's gold, and Douglas will be dead."

"He gave me his gold for safekeeping. He was afraid Finn would steal it."

"Jack Finn?"

Lopaka nodded.

"Little William thinks Finn killed the doctor," I said.

"How do you know Little William?"

"Tomorrow, when we are at Reverend Newhouse's, Doctor Douglas's body will be examined, and Little William tells everyone Finn did it."

"No." Lopaka shook his head. "The doctor's still at our camp." He walked to the cliff and pointed to the camp.

"It's there," Lopaka said.

But the morning fog was so dense, all I could see was a silver haze. "Listen!" I heard men arguing.

Lopaka cocked his ear toward the sound. "It's Finn and the doctor."

"I'm not lying," I said. "He's going to kill Douglas."

"How could you know this?" He stared at me.

"I'm telling you the truth. You've got to save him."

Lopaka ran down the trail, and before I could tell him anything else, he was gone. Took off. Like a hurdler. He leaped over tree roots and pivoted around boulders. When he turned down the first switchback, I could only catch a glimpse of him through the trees.

Maybe this was all I had to do? Warn Lopaka about Finn, then Lopaka rescues Douglas, and there is no murder. No trial. And the Kekoa curse will be over.

I thought my part of the bargain was done and I waited to be transported home, but nothing happened.

I still couldn't see Lopaka in the woods. Maybe I'm supposed to help him rescue Douglas? We both fight Finn? But what could I do? I was a skinny, sixth-grade kid. Lopaka was the strong one.

Maybe I had to witness it? Be there when he rescued Douglas?

I hiked down the trail. It was easy at first, wide and smooth. Then at the first switchback, it narrowed. At the next switchback, the path was no more than a ledge the width of my foot.

I shimmied around a curve, holding on to a tree branch. The farther down the trail I went, the more it narrowed until the only things I could step on were jutting tree roots sticking out of the cliff.

It was a sheer drop. If I fell, no one would ever find my body.

I thought about turning back. Then I remembered Blaise calling me a coward. If Blaise were there, he'd follow Lopaka. He'd be right behind him, ready to fight hand-to-hand.

Keep going, I told myself. You're not a coward.

As I hiked down, the fog lifted and I could see the clearing and a dog that was barking.

"Shut up, you mutt." It had to be Finn's voice.

But the dog kept barking.

"Shut up!"

The dog strained at his leash, up on its hind legs, barking at a man who was hunched over a body.

The body had to be David Douglas. We were too late.

"Where is it?" Finn's voice was loud and gravelly. "You know I'll find it." He rummaged through backpacks and boxes and flung tapa bundles and a brass telescope.

Douglas mumbled an answer. He wasn't dead! He propped himself up on his elbow and answered again, but I couldn't understand what he said.

"Shut up!" Finn threw a notebook at the dog. He tore open a canvas bag, picked up bodies of birds, and tossed them away.

"Not my specimens!" Douglas reached his hand out. "Please!" he pleaded.

A hawk flew overhead. It screeched and soared, and Finn picked up the telescope off the ground and followed its flight. The hawk flew in my direction. I was sure Finn would see me. I didn't move. I held my breath. The hawk dipped and soared, then flew over the mountain, and Finn threw the telescope on the ground.

"Tell me where the gold is." Finn ripped through tapa

bundles, spilling out plants and leaves.

"I told you, I don't have any gold."

"You said you were booking a ship's passage to London. How were you going to pay for that? With specimens?"

"The British Horticultural Society pays my bills," Douglas said. "I collect plants for them, and they pay my expenses."

The dog kept barking.

"I told you, shut up." Finn kicked the dog.

"Billie!" Douglas screamed.

Finn drew his knife from his belt and flicked his thumb on its blade. "It would be a shame if the little mutt died."

"The dog's done nothing to you." Douglas crawled toward Billie on his hands and knees, but just before Douglas got to Billie, Finn snatched the dog in his arm and pressed the knife against Billie's neck. "Which will it be, doctor? The dog or the gold?"

"I told you I have no gold."

Finn pressed the knife into the dog's neck, burying it in its fur.

"All right! The gold is with my guide."

"Lopaka Aiona?"

"Yes." Douglas nodded and reached out for the dog. "Now give me Billie."

"Not yet. Where's Aiona?"

"I don't know."

Finn pressed the blade harder against Billie's neck, and a small bead of blood appeared.

"It's true," Douglas yelled. "I sent him to find a trail to Hilo. One that you wouldn't follow."

Finn kept a grip on the dog. "What else?"

"Even if you find him, the truth is there's not much gold left. Almost all of it's been spent."

Finn handed Billie to Douglas, and Douglas cradled the dog and kissed it on its head.

"What about this stuff?" Finn waved his hand over Douglas's

things. "Is anything worth money?"

Douglas looked around. "The telescope."

Finn threw his knife on the ground; it twirled and landed upright a few feet from Douglas. "You see how kind I am?" He laughed. "I could have aimed for your heart."

Finn picked up the telescope and bounced it in his hands as if he were weighing it. "How much money could I get for this?"

"Several pounds," Douglas said. "A ship's captain would pay more." As he answered Finn, Douglas eyed Finn's knife.

Finn held the telescope to his eye and scanned the cliffs. He had his back to Douglas.

"See how powerful it is." Douglas crept toward the knife. "You can even see birds hidden in the trees."

Finn adjusted the focus on the telescope.

"Keep adjusting it," Douglas said. "The lens is German made." His voice was calm and even. "It's the best in the world." Douglas got to the knife. He crawled to his knees, then stood up. "At night you can see the stars," Douglas said.

Finn scanned the sky, and Douglas heaved the knife over his head and lunged at Finn. Finn turned around! He side-stepped Douglas, and the doctor fell forward.

"Fool!" Finn bashed Douglas with the telescope.

Douglas's head jerked back.

Finn hit him again.

The doctor collapsed on the ground, and Finn hit him again.

Douglas's body shuddered, and Finn struck him one last time.

I knew Doctor Douglas was dead.

Finn fell to his knees and rocked back and forth, wailing, rocking. I felt sorry for him. He didn't plan to kill Douglas. He saw the knife and panicked.

Finn's sobbing got louder, but it wasn't grief I heard, it was laughter. Finn had just killed Douglas, and he was laughing.

"High and mighty, Doctor Douglas." Finn cackled. "If you had only played cards with me, you'd still be breathing."

Finn dug through Douglas's pockets. Finding nothing, he pulled off the doctor's boot, turned it upside down, and shook it. When there was nothing in it, he took off the other boot. Again, there was nothing.

Then Finn lifted Douglas's hand. I saw the glint of a gold ring on Douglas's finger and knew what would happen next. I remembered Mr. Wilcocks holding up Douglas's severed hand.

Finn reached for a rock and placed it under Douglas's hand. He spread the doctor's fingers. He straddled Douglas's arm and gripped the knife in his hands.

I turned away.

I heard the clang of metal against rock.

When I turned back, Finn was wiping his bloodied knife on his trousers and Billie was barking.

Finn tugged the ring off the severed finger, then he spit on the ring, wiped it off on his shirt, and stuffed it in his pants pocket. Then he walked toward Billie.

"You're next." He raised his knife.

"No!" I screamed.

Finn looked up. "Lopaka, is that you?"

I froze. I knew if Finn found me, it wouldn't matter who I was, he'd kill me too.

Finn stood still, looked up toward me, then went back to Douglas's body, searching every pocket of his clothes a second time, and when he didn't find anything, he kicked the doctor in the back.

I heard someone running up the trail.

CHAPTER NINE

It was Lopaka.

"It's just as you said. Finn killed the doctor." Lopaka was panting. "I couldn't get down there fast enough to save him."

"Finn thinks you're up here," I said. "When I thought he was going to kill the dog, I screamed."

Lopaka didn't say anything. He walked to the edge of the cliff.

"What do we do now?" I asked.

"I don't know."

Noah followed Lopaka. From there he could see Finn dragging Douglas's body by the ankles.

"What's he doing?"

"The bull pit is there." Lopaka pointed to a patch of vines about forty yards away. "He's going to dump the body."

As Finn dragged the doctor's body, Douglas's arms dangled like a rag doll's, and his head bounced on the stones.

"Can't we tell Reverend Newhouse what happened now? Before we get captured?"

Lopaka held up the pouch with the gold in it.

"Just toss it," I said.

"It will still be missing."

"So what?"

"No one will believe I wasn't there when he was killed. I'm

his guide. I'm never supposed to leave him."

"Maybe we could tell Little William?"

"No."

Then, at the edge of the clearing, I saw a flash of someone running out of the woods, but when it emerged, it looked like a walking thatched hut. "What is that?"

"It's Kia Manu."

"Your aunt?" The figure wore a long cape of dried leaves that hung from her neck to her knees.

"She lives up the next ridge. She must have heard the fight."

Finn didn't look up. He was intent on dragging Douglas's body as Kia Manu brazenly walked into the open field. She knelt over the scattered boxes and bundles, then she methodically opened each box and unwrapped each tapa bundle.

"Why don't you let her know you're here?" I asked.

He said, "I will," but he didn't. He kept watching her go through Douglas's stuff. She picked up the birds, examined them, stuffed some into her sling, and tossed the others.

"We can hike to the edge of the clearing, so she can see us," I said.

"And so will Finn." Lopaka waited until Finn was farther away from Kia Manu when, finally, he called out to her. He pinched his nostrils, opened his mouth wide, and screeched like a hawk.

Kia Manu looked up, scanned the mountain, then went back to her scavenging.

"Do it again," I said.

"Patience."

What was he waiting for? Finn was pulling at a patch of vines, exposing a pit about six feet wide.

"It's the bull trap," Lopaka said.

After Finn cleared the vines, he knelt behind Doctor Douglas's body and rolled it into the pit! There was a thud and moaning. "The doctor's still alive!"

"No. It's the bull," Lopaka said.

I thought of the bulls at the rodeos, bucking and stomping their riders. What if Douglas wasn't dead? Could he feel every gore of the bull?

Lopaka put his hands to his mouth and screeched like a hawk again.

Kia Manu answered his call. Then the two of them went back and forth with their bird noises, sounding like a conversation.

Finn stood up, put his hands on his hips, and leaned backward. Then he wiped the sweat from his forehead with his hand and spotted Kia Manu. "Thief!" He yelled.

Kia Manu looked straight at him.

"Thief!"

Kia Manu didn't react. She walked over to Billie, untied him, and cradled him in her arms, and disappeared into the woods.

"Get out of here, old woman!" Finn waved his hat in the air.

That's when I saw Finn's face, the gray shark eyes. Finn and Shaggy were the same man!

"Let's go," Lopaka said. "Kia Manu told me where to meet her."

I grabbed his arm. "Finn lives in my time too."

"Alive?"

"Ghost or real. He's there."

"You've been in the future. What happens next?" Lopaka asked.

"The next thing I remember is that we're tied up, and we're marching up the hill with hunters and cowboys until we get to Reverend Newhouse's."

"And the reverend helps us." It was more of a question than a statement.

I shook my head. "He doesn't think we killed Douglas, but a lot of other men do."

"Why?"

"I told you. They found you with Douglas's gold."

"He gave me his gold because he was afraid Finn would steal it." Lopaka paced. "The doctor liked spending time with fellow Englishmen, so when Finn invited him for supper, he accepted. But as soon as we got to Finn's house, I knew it was a bad decision.

"Finn met us at the gate; he smelled of alcohol and slurred his words. He walked us to his house, and the doctor told me to wait outside with Billie. So, I sat on the ground, close enough to hear what was going on inside.

"Then a woman came out of the smokehouse, carrying a platter of sweet potatoes, poi, and pork. Before she went into Finn's house, she squatted in front of me and gave Billy a bone and me some pork.

"At first, things between Finn and the doctor sounded friendly. Then Finn's voice got louder, and I heard him challenge the doctor to play a game of cards, but the doctor refused. Finn challenged him again, louder. I looked through the window and saw the doctor get up to leave. He told Finn he had a long hike in the morning and he needed his rest.

"Then Finn accused the doctor of thinking he was too good to play cards with him, and when the doctor denied it, Finn pushed him, and the doctor stumbled. That's when I ran inside.

"I punched Finn, not that hard, but he was so drunk he collapsed on the floor and passed out.

"We were supposed to stay the night at Finn's, but the doctor said we had to make camp away from him. I told the doctor I knew about a clearing about half mile away where we could make camp.

"He agreed and we set out, but as we hiked, it got darker, and the doctor stopped more frequently. He told me to take Billie and go ahead, that he would catch up. I told him I didn't want to leave him, but he insisted his eyesight was too poor to walk any faster during the night.

"I made camp and tied Billie to a tree. When the doctor

arrived, I had his evening tea ready, and as I did every night, I massaged his feet with kukui nut oil. While I rubbed his feet, the doctor told me he was afraid Finn would follow us. I asked if he wanted to break camp again and hike a few more miles up the trail, but he said he couldn't because his vision was so bad, he could only see shadows.

"He told me to stay with him through the night, but at dawn, I should scout out a trail to Hilo. He said, 'One that Finn wouldn't expect us to use.' Then he gave me his gold for safe-keeping." Lopaka paused. "That's why I have his gold."

"Now what?" I asked.

"I meet Kia Manu."

"OK, let's go."

"I'm going alone. You couldn't keep up with me."

"At least let me try."

"There's a lava tube near here. You can wait for me there."

I had no choice but to follow Lopaka up a trail to a T where it split. In front of us was a stone cliff with a curtain of vines hanging from it. Lopaka pulled back the vines to expose a cave.

"Come on," he said.

It was dark and slippery.

I slid my hand along the wall as I walked. The deeper in the cave, the cooler it got.

"Lopaka?"

"Keep going," Lopaka answered.

There was a strong smell of vinegar, and I saw gourds hanging from the walls. When I caught up to Lopaka, he was piling tapa blankets on the ground. "When the tapa makers come, they'll have food to share with you."

Why would I need food? "How long will you be gone?"

"A few days," he said. "Just stay deep in the cave and wait."

I wanted to beg him to take me with him, but I knew it wouldn't do any good.

Lopaka left me, and I sat on the blankets with my knees

crossed and my head in my hands. What if he doesn't come back? What if Finn catches up to him and he never gets to Kia Manu? What will happen to me then?

I remembered Mr. Goodall talking about that boy's body that was found in the cave. They weren't 100 percent sure it was Lopaka. It was just the body of a boy about Lopaka's age. Maybe that boy was me?

"Noah." A gray figure took shape in front of me, then colors appeared, and I saw a red T-shirt.

I stood up to get a better look. But what if I was seeing another ghost? "How do I know it's you?"

He came closer. The face was Papa's for sure, but I was still uncertain.

"Tell me something that only my Papa would know," I said.

"Do you remember your first day at kindergarten when you held on to my shirt and wouldn't let go? I had to carry you into class. Do you remember that?"

"That happens to lots of kids," I said.

"I gave you a cat's eye marble and told you to put it in your pocket, so whenever you got scared, you could rub it and know I was waiting to pick you up."

"It is you!" I hugged him.

He took me in his arms. "*Aloha au iā ʻoe*, Noah." I love you.

He rocked me, and I held on to him tightly and sobbed. "Papa, what's happening to me?"

"Do you remember the time at the dump when the Night Marchers came down the valley?"

"That was a dream."

"It was real," he said. "That night you promised a Night Marcher that you would save someone in his family."

"I was only four. How could I make a promise like that?"

"You looked at the Night Marcher and he was going to take you with him. I tried to get him to take me instead, but he wouldn't. Instead, I bargained to let you go, and he agreed if you would save someone in his family."

"But I was only four."

Papa didn't say anything.

"Is it true that if I don't save Lopaka I'll die the same day?"

"I don't know," Papa said. "The only way we can be sure is if you save Lopaka."

"Why can't you save him?"

"The Night Marcher chose you."

"What if you send me home?"

"You may die there too."

"Send me home, Papa. It's a better chance than I have here."

"I don't know."

If Papa didn't send me home, he was condemning me to die. Well, I thought, if my trick worked on Lopaka, maybe it would work on Papa too. "If you send me home, I can find proof that Lopaka's innocent. Blaise can help me. We can go on the internet or get some librarian to help us find stuff."

He didn't answer.

"Papa, it's the only way."

"Promise me you'll find a way to save Lopaka."

Look what he made me promise already!

I said, "I promise," but I wasn't sure if I would.

CHAPTER TEN

Papa sent me home. I was back in the cemetery.

Blaise and Mr. Goodall were near the shed, taking stuff out of a shopping cart and sorting it into piles. Blankets and yoga mats went in one wheelbarrow and canned food and bottled water in another.

I looked for Finn but didn't see him.

"Over here." Blaise waved to me.

As I got to the shed, Mr. Goodall asked me if I had found my phone. I looked at Blaise for an answer.

"I told Mr. Goodall that you thought you lost your phone when we were on the service project and that we came back to look for it."

"Oh, yeah." I patted the back pocket of my jeans. "Found it."

"I was telling Mr. Goodall about the History Day contest." Blaise stared at me wide-eyed, as if he were sending me some kind of telepathic message. "You know . . . the video we're making."

"I think you've got yourselves a winning project," Mr. Goodall said, then his phone rang. "'Who Killed David Douglas? The Story Behind the Story.' Impressive title." The phone rang again, and Mr. Goodall put his finger in the air and took the call.

"What video?" I whispered to Blaise.

"I told him after we listened to his talk, we decided to do a video about who killed Douglas."

It was amazing how easily Blaise could lie.

Mr. Goodall ended the call. "That was the roofers. They're on their way over with an estimate to patch around the steeple." He looked at where the shingles were missing. "I have a feeling it's going to be pricey."

I smiled.

"If you boys don't mind giving me a hand, I'd like to finish up before they get here."

"What do you want us to do?" I asked.

"Somehow, this shopping cart turned into a makeshift donation center and every few days I sort it out and put the usable things in the Outreach Center."

"I thought the cart belonged to the homeless guy," I said.

"Which homeless guy?" Mr. Goodall laughed. "We have quite a few who live here—characters all of them—even the dead ones." Goodall pointed to a gravestone with a heart, club, diamond, and spade carved into the base. "Finn Jackson. Born London, England, 1802. Died Honolulu, 1878. The story goes he played poker with King Kamehameha III."

Finn Jackson had to be Jack Finn!

"Then there's the boy with the boat." He jutted his chin at a statue of a small boy holding a sailboat. "He died playing in the Nuʻuanu Stream."

Mr. Goodall's phone rang again. "OK. I'll be right there." He turned to us. "The roofers are here. They must have been right down the street when they called." He stuffed his phone in his pocket. "Would you boys mind putting these things in the church basement? I should be back in a few minutes."

"No worries," Blaise said.

As soon as Mr. Goodall was out of earshot, Blaise apologized, "Noah, I'm really sorry I pushed you to go back to the past."

It seemed like so long ago, and so much had happened

since, I didn't even remember how I returned to Lopaka's time.

"I didn't mean what I said."

I held my hand up. "Forget it."

"But, cuz—"

"Listen to me! We've got bigger problems. The homeless guy is Jack Finn."

"Jack Finn, the guy from the past?"

Finn appeared in front of us! "I can assure you, boys, that I am all of them."

"Do you see him?" I whispered to Blaise.

"All six feet of him," Blaise said.

"What do you want?" I asked Finn.

"I'm here to protect you," he said. "You need to know the truth about how Douglas died. It was Lopaka Aiona who killed him, not me."

"I saw you do it!" I said.

"You saw what Lopaka showed you."

"Kia Manu was there. She saw you too."

"There is no Kia Manu. Lopaka is tricking you."

"What about Little William and Reverend Newhouse? They think you're a murderer."

Finn shook his head. "There is no Little William or Reverend Newhouse."

"My Papa was there. He wouldn't lie to me."

"None of what you saw was real," Finn said.

"If it didn't happen, then how do you know about it?"

"Noah, I'm telling you the truth. If you go back to the past, Lopaka will abandon you, and you'll be the one who's hanged."

"Lopaka wouldn't do that."

"Did he leave you in the cave?" Finn asked.

"He made sure I was safe."

"I'm warning you: he'll abandon you again, and the next time, you'll hang." Then Finn disappeared.

Blaise looked at me. "Did that just happen?"

I nodded.

"That was him? Jack Finn?"

"Yeah."

"Could what he said about Lopaka be right?"

"No way! I saw him kill Douglas with my own eyes."

"How do you know it was real?"

"I saw it!"

"You asked me to believe you traveled back 200 years. Why's it so hard for you to believe that Finn might be telling the truth?

"Because I was there, and you weren't!" I tossed the blankets in the wheelbarrow. "Or are you going to tell me what I saw?" I plowed past him toward the church.

I hated that Blaise might be right. No, he can't be, I thought. Lopaka wouldn't do that to me. Besides, Papa was there and only he would have known about my first day at kindergarten. It had to be Papa.

Blaise and I waited for Mr. Goodall in front of the basement steps. Blaise walked back and forth, and I sat on the top step. Neither of us spoke. We didn't even look at each other.

Mr. Goodall headed toward us. "That was quicker than I thought, and the roof's not going to be half as expensive as I expected. Today is a good day."

Maybe for him, it was.

I followed Goodall into the basement. The brick stairs were crumbling. The wrought iron handrails were flaked and the door at the bottom looked like it was straight out of a dungeon. Mr. Goodall put a long iron key in the lock and pushed on the door, but it didn't budge. Then he put his shoulder into it and rammed it until it opened. Judging from the groove marks on the stone floor, the door must have been a problem for a long time.

"Come on in, boys."

Mr. Goodall flipped on the lights and a row of naked light bulbs, dangling from thick black wires, flickered.

I followed him in and breathed my first whiff of mildew and bug spray.

"This is your archive?" Blaise asked.

"It's a low-budget operation," Mr. Goodall said.

"More like no budget," Blaise said.

"Where do you want me to put these blankets?" I asked.

He pointed to a tower of Rubbermaid bins stacked right in front of the exit door. Each bin was labeled with a "Hello My Name Is" tag with "Outreach/Food" scribbled on it.

Blaise and I looked at each other. Both of us were sons of firefighters. For our whole lives, our fathers drummed into us to always look for the exits when we were in a new place.

"You know you can't block an exit?" Blaise said.

"That door's been boarded up for years," Mr. Goodall said.

"Where's the emergency exit?" I asked.

"I guess that's it." He pointed to a small window over a cafeteria table.

"So, there's only one way in and one way out?" I asked.

"I guess so. But it's not that big a place." He laughed.

I estimated the basement to be ten feet by twenty feet, not big, but still, there was only one way in and out.

"If I had time, I'd let you boys look at the Douglas stuff now, but I've got another meeting scheduled, fundraising stuff, but I'm free at nine tomorrow morning," he directed his words at Blaise. "Do you want to meet then?"

"We'll be here," Blaise said.

When we were back at our bikes, I said, "I'm not coming back here." I swiveled my head, looking for Finn.

"We've got to find proof Lopaka didn't do it," Blaise said. "We've got to save Papa."

"I thought you believed Finn, and that Lopaka made the whole thing up. What if I didn't see Papa? What if Lopaka made him up too?"

"No matter," he said. "You went to the past, and the curse is real. Now we've got to fix it." Blaise looked around. "Finn's a ghost, right?"

"I don't know what he is."

"If he's a ghost, he can't hurt us, right?"

"I'm not counting on it," I said.

"But he couldn't do anything to us in broad daylight. Not with everybody watching."

"Except that no one else can see him but you and me."

And almost like he heard us, Finn appeared. "That's right, Noah. No one else can see me. But I can see you and I can hear you too." He gripped the handlebars of my bike. "I heard you boys tell Mr. Goodall you'll be coming back tomorrow."

"So what?" Blaise acted brave, but I could tell when he was scared.

"Leave it alone, Blaise," I said.

Blaise kept pushing. "If you didn't kill Douglas, you should be glad we're going through all the stuff, then we'll prove Lopaka did it."

"None of this is your *kuleana*," Finn said.

"Come on, Blaise. Let's go home."

"Your cousin's a wise man. Go home," Finn said.

Finn let go of my handlebars and I got on my bike.

Finn grinned at Blaise. "Be careful, boy, before you end up dead too."

Blaise glared at Finn as he mounted his bike.

CHAPTER ELEVEN

We rode out of the cemetery, pumping on our pedals, kicking up gravel, swerving and leaning, and screeching out of the church driveway onto King Street.

I looked back and saw Finn standing at the cemetery gate. Blaise was right behind me. We sped past the Salvation Army and the shave ice store, down our street, past the condos, then the houses, and into my driveway where we pulled into the carport, stomped on our brakes, and sat on our bikes, panting, heads down, our sweat dripping on the concrete.

"You OK?" I asked.

Blaise nodded. "Do you think Finn can follow us?"

"I don't think he can leave the cemetery."

"Right," Blaise agreed, although I could tell by the tone of his voice he wasn't convinced either.

I opened the screen door and called out to my sister, "Tia, you home?"

No answer.

"Tia?"

No answer.

"She must be at track practice," I said. "We lucked out."

Blaise followed me into my room and sat on my computer chair, rolled it over, and put his feet on my bed.

I propped pillows against my headboard and plopped myself down.

"No matter what he is, Finn's a pretty scary guy," Blaise said.

"Yeah, and you were talking pretty big."

"I do that." Blaise shrugged.

"I don't know what to do," I said. "He's here and he's there. Maybe I really will die the same day as Lopaka. What if Finn kills me?"

There was a knock on the door, and before I could say, "Come in," Tia walked in with her hands on her hips and wearing her Roosevelt High School track team shirt.

"Oh, pah-leese, come in," I said.

Tia ignored my sarcasm.

"Where have you been? I messaged you twice."

I wanted to say that there wasn't great cell reception back in 1834.

She flicked her hair over her shoulder. "The four of them are going to be late."

She meant Blaise's parents and ours.

"The dads are at the station setting up for the chili drive and 'The Sisters' are shopping for it. They left money for us to order food. Or . . ." She jingled car keys over her head. "We could go out."

"With you driving? No, thanks," I said.

"I'm going to Pearl Ridge."

"My life's dream! Cruising the mall with my sister on a Friday night."

"At least she's not babysitting us," Blaise said.

I had no idea what Blaise was talking about. We hadn't been babysat for years.

"My best babysitter was Grandma Kekoa," he said.

"Sorry, Blaise, I'm not the grandmother type," Tia sniped.

"Did Grandma ever babysit you?" Blaise asked.

"No. I was older when they moved to town."

"So, you missed all her stories?"

"You mean about growing up in the country and hunting pigs?"

"Those and the one about the Kekoa curse. Did she tell you that one?"

"You mean the family cover-up?" Tia asked.

"What cover-up?" I asked.

"You're talking about the Night Marcher story about Papa taking you to the dump?"

Blaise and I looked at each other.

"You two don't know, do you?"

"Know what?" I asked.

"Oh, you poor innocent babes." Tia moved my leg over and sat on the bed. "I guess it's time you heard it." She took a deep breath. "Once upon a time, when Papa babysat Noah, he took him up to Dump Road." Tia looked at me. "Papa brought you back really late, and when you got back, you had a burn on your hand, and Mom had a fit!

"Mom and Papa argued. Mom was screaming about Papa being irresponsible, then Dad stepped in and said it was just a bruise. Then Mom and Dad fought, and she yelled that he didn't care that you got burned at the dump, and she zoomed you off to the emergency room. The rest of us piled in Dad's car and followed her.

"It took hours before the doctors finally saw you. When they did, they said they didn't know what was on your hand, but they said it wasn't a burn.

"The next day, Mom took you to Doctor Fujimoto, and he said sometimes birthmarks don't appear until a child is three or four years old. But Mom wasn't buying it. She was sure something happened at the dump. She was so mad she didn't talk to Papa for weeks." Tia's phone pinged, but she kept on with the story. "It wasn't a happy place around here! After a while, Tutu came up with the Night Marchers story." Tia drew her breath in as if she were going to say something, then stopped.

"Then what?" I asked.

"Papa died a few months after that, and I don't think he and Mom ever worked things out. So, I wouldn't go around asking her about it."

"Do you think the Night Marcher story was true?" Blaise asked.

"Um." She smirked. "That would be a 'no.'"

"Sometimes I have a dream about Papa and the Night Marchers," I said.

"And I definitely wouldn't tell Mom that!" she said.

"Uncle Solomon says that dreams are real," Blaise said. "He says they're messages from our ancestors."

"Yeah, and the voices get louder the bigger the audience he has." Tia rolled her eyes.

"My mom says Uncle Solomon is a dream interpreter," Blaise said.

"Well, my family doesn't believe in that stuff," Tia said, and she was right. Mom said all the "old ways stories" were good for just that: stories. And until that morning, I had agreed with her.

Tia's phone pinged again, and she read the text, "Nicole's meeting me at the mall." She shoved her phone into her jeans pocket. "There's money on the kitchen counter when you two figure out what you want to order. I'm off to the mall." She threw us a kiss.

After she left, Blaise said, "Your mother's wrong about Uncle Solomon. He knows about the old ways," Blaise said. "He can tell us how to prove Lopaka isn't a murderer."

"If there is any proof, it's going to be in the cemetery archive," I said.

"What if we don't find anything there?" Blaise asked.

"We will."

"But if we don't. Will you promise me to Uncle Solomon?"

"Sure," I said, but I knew that wasn't going to happen.

CHAPTER TWELVE

That night I had the dream again. In the dream, I saw Papa drive down Dump Road. The shoulders on both sides were piled with abandoned cars, washing machines, sinks, mattresses, and plywood and any other stuff that never made it to the pay-by-the-pound dump.

It was still light out when Papa pulled over and parked his pickup next to an abandoned couch.

"Too bad it's ripped," Papa said as he carried me out of the truck and set me on the ground. "I could put that in my work shed." Then, like every other time we went to the dump, he said, "Let's go on a treasure hunt." That night, he was looking for a Volkswagen hubcap.

He scouted under bushes and through junk piles. "It used to be I'd come down here just like a store and pick up whatever I needed. Now, I gotta work for it."

"You know your letters, Noah?"

"Some."

"You know *V* and *W*?"

"Sometimes," I said.

He picked up a hubcap, then tossed it back. He wasn't having any luck, so we went deeper into the valley where the trees covered what little light there was.

"Can we go home now, Papa?" I was afraid of the dark and

I was afraid of anything in the dark.

"Just a little more." Papa told me to sit on a rock and wait.

I waited and I waited. I made circles in the dirt with a twig. Then a mongoose ran in front of me. "Papa!"

"It's just a mongoose." Papa laughed.

"But it was big."

"Big as a lion?" he asked.

"Not that big."

"Big as a dog?"

"No."

"Small as a mongoose?"

I nodded.

"Then I can protect you." He went back to searching.

A minute later, I asked, "Can we go now, Papa?"

"Not yet."

"When?"

"Five more minutes."

"It stinks." I sniffed the air. It smelled like rotten fruit and cane fire. I pulled my T-shirt over my nose. "I want to go home."

A conch shell blew, and Papa cocked his head. "Hush!"

Then I heard the drumming of *ipu*.

"Get on the ground," Papa yelled at me.

"Why?"

"Just do it!"

The drumming got louder, and I heard men chanting.

Papa lay on the ground next to me and put his arm around my shoulders. "Close your eyes, Noah, and keep them closed."

I felt the words of the chant bang through my chest. I looked up and saw warriors taller than the sky floating in fire.

"Don't look!" Papa pushed my face into the dirt.

I shut my eyes, but I could feel the wind whirling. I turned my head and snuck a look. The warriors wore gourd helmets. Some of them carried clubs studded with shark teeth, others had long javelins.

A warrior stopped in front of me. His *malo* was stained with blood and his leg was marked with a shark tooth tattoo.

I looked up at him. He had glowing orange eyes.

Papa pressed my head down, but I strained against him.

"It is forbidden!" the Night Marcher screamed, and when he spoke, the ground shook and flames swirled around me.

Papa screamed, "No!"

The line of warriors chanted, "O-ia!" Let him be pierced and death will follow.

The wind lifted me.

Papa held his hand out to me. "Grab my hand."

I couldn't reach him.

"Noah!" Papa screamed.

I was blown into the Night Marcher's arms.

"He's mine," the Night Marcher said.

Papa begged him, "Leave the boy. Take me."

The Night Marcher held me tighter. He said, "It's forbidden to look at a Night Marcher." His breath smelled of spoiled meat.

"It's my fault," Papa said. "I never taught him the old ways."

"If you know the old ways, old man, then you know he must die."

"Let him live!"

"Help me, Papa!"

"He's my grandson." Papa was crying.

The Night Marcher loosened his grip.

"I'll do anything if you spare him." Papa was on his knees.

"If I spare him, he will be in my debt."

"But he's just a child," Papa said.

"Then he will die a child." When the Night Marcher spoke, the flames grew taller.

"Whatever you want, I'll do it." Papa sobbed.

"He is *na'u*." The Night Marcher took my hand and a beam shot from his eyes and burned a mark into my palm. "*Na'u*." He is mine.

The flames died down. "There will be a time when one of my family will be falsely accused of murder and sentenced to die. This child must save him. And if he doesn't, the two boys will die the same day, and your spirit, old man, will never rest in peace."

"He will do it. I swear."

"It's not your *kuleana*. The boy must swear."

"Say the words, Noah. Tell him you swear to save his grandson."

In my dream, I watched as the four-year-old me said, "I swear."

The Night Marcher let go of me and I floated down into Papa's arms.

"Forgive me." Papa held me tight. "Forgive me." He sobbed. "*Aloha au iā 'oe*," I love you.

Papa cradled me and the Night Marchers drifted into the fire and marched to the sea.

CHAPTER THIRTEEN

When I woke up, I looked at my hand and stared at the mark. Trying to deny what happened wasn't an option. The mark was right there. The story was true.

I heard my mom yell at Tia. "You're always late," she said. "I have to pick up Auntie Sophie now, not five minutes from now. I'll come back for you." I heard the screen door slam.

I checked my phone. It was nine o'clock, and I was already late to meet Blaise at the cemetery.

I jumped out of bed, got dressed, and grabbed the pouch.

Tia was in the kitchen, licking *malasada* sugar off her fingers. "Where are you going?"

"Out."

"And when Mom asks me where you are, what am I supposed to say?"

"I'm at the basketball court with Blaise."

By the time I got to the cemetery, Blaise was in the archive, sitting on the floor surrounded by boxes, ziplock bags, and piles of newspapers.

"Sorry, I'm late."

"No worries." Blaise pushed some boxes out of the way and motioned for me to sit.

There was hardly any room; everywhere there were plastic bins, blankets, old flags, furniture, and plain junk.

"This place is a firetrap," I said.

"Yeah, and it's full of centipedes." He reached back for a piece of cardboard. "Sit on this. At least it'll keep your butt dry."

"Did you find anything?" I shoved the cardboard under myself.

Blaise handed me a brittle, yellowed paper. "It's a letter Douglas wrote to his brother two days before he died." Blaise pointed to the bottom of the page. "Read the last paragraph."

The writing was squiggly and old-fashioned and some of the ink was smudged. I read it out loud: "I am plagued with an inflammation of the right eye, and my left is blinded by the sun. There are some days I only see shadows, and everything is gray. I fear I am losing my sight."

Blaise asked me if I thought Douglas could have accidentally fallen in the pit because he didn't see it.

For a second, I wondered too, but then I remembered. "No, I saw it. I watched Finn dump his body in the pit."

"Right," Blaise said, but there was something in his voice that sounded like he didn't totally believe me.

The two of us worked until the church bells chimed eleven. Neither of us found anything worthwhile. The best thing I found was a pennant from the 1963 World's Fair.

"This is useless," I said. "Maybe those research guys took all the good stuff already."

"Mr. Goodall said there's more stuff up there." Blaise pointed to the cardboard boxes on a shelf that was nailed to the rafters.

"Did he say how we're going to get up there?" The shelf was about ten feet from the floor.

"He said he was going to get a ladder, but that was when he first got here, and he never came back."

"Did he say anything else?"

Blaise laughed. "He said, 'Try not to get hurt or break anything.'"

"Or electrocuted?" I was sitting on wet cardboard under dangling light bulbs that kept flickering off and on.

"I'll check the maintenance shed for a ladder," Blaise said.

I didn't go with him. I looked around for another way to get to the shelves.

There was a cafeteria table pushed against the wall. If we stood on it, maybe we could reach the shelf, but I wasn't sure if it could hold us. I leaned on it, shook it, and climbed up on it. Then I bounced up and down and the table held.

Standing on the table, I was high enough to see out the basement window. Well, I might have been able to see out if it weren't for the soot and the spiderwebs.

I rubbed my fist against the pane, but that just smeared the soot worse. So, I spit on the window and wiped it again. It was clear enough for me to see Blaise coming back from the shed.

"I couldn't find any ladder," he said, coming down the steps.

"We don't need it. Come on up." I reached my hand out to pull him up to the table.

The shelf was still about nine inches beyond our reach.

"What if I give you a boost?" Blaise cupped his hands and pushed me up high enough to crawl onto the shelf. The shelf was about three feet from the ceiling, and when I crawled on my hands and knees, I scraped my back on the rafters.

There must have been twenty boxes up there, all cardboard, all water-stained, and sagging.

"What do you see?" Blaise asked.

I read the label on the first box, "Budget reports: 1870-1895." The second box was the same.

Blaise cupped his hand to the window.

"You see anything out there?" I asked.

"There's no sign of Finn, if that's what you're asking."

"Keep looking," I said.

I shifted around more boxes and read the labels: "1941-1945. Boy Scout Awards. Aloha Parade 1985. Maybe Goodall's wrong," I said. "There's nothing up here."

"You give up too easy," Blaise said.

"I do not!"

I crawled into the back corner and shoved around some more boxes and spotted the prize. "I found it!" I read the label, "Missionary Journals. Letters. David Douglas. Miscellaneous."

I scooted backward, dragging the box, then pushed it to the edge of the shelf and tilted it. "You got it?" I asked Blaise. "It's heavy."

"Got it."

I slid the box off the shelf and Blaise reached for it. The box dropped, then bounced onto the floor, splitting open, spilling out books and ladies' dresses.

"You got it? Nice job," I said.

"You pushed it too fast," he said, looking at the mess on the floor.

Blaise helped me down, and we jumped off the table and rummaged through the boxes. They were full of dresses, a silver mirror, shoeboxes tied with twine, old newspapers, and silverfish—hundreds of silverfish.

"I found Abagail Newhouse's journal," he said. "Listen. 'July 13, 1834. Mother made scones and *poha* jelly to celebrate the arrival of Doctor Douglas, but he never arrived. Instead of the day he was supposed to visit us, he died. Some said he was murdered, and Papa had his murderers sleeping in the *hale*!'"

Blaise looked up. "She underlined it three times. Then she wrote, 'I heard Mother and Father talk about the murderers, but Father said the boys were innocent. He thought Jack Finn was the murderer. How am I supposed to go to sleep knowing there are murderers right outside my door?'

"Mother chastised Father, saying he shouldn't talk of such things." Then Blaise said, "The rest of it is junk. She wrote she was angry with Douglas because he promised to bring her a mirror from London." Blaise shut the journal. "Right. He's dead, and she's mad about a mirror."

We kept searching.

We found old newspapers, accounting ledgers, and Farmer's Almanacs, but there was nothing about Douglas.

A shadow flickered past the window. "Did you see that?" I asked.

Blaise shook his head. "It was probably a cat."

I climbed up on the table to look out the window.

"Do you see anything?" Blaise asked.

"No, but that doesn't mean that Finn isn't here." I climbed back down, but every few seconds, I glanced back up at the window.

"Maybe we should shut the door," I said.

"Mr. Goodall left it open," Blaise said.

But Mr. Goodall wasn't worried about Jack Finn.

I went back to rifling through stuff in the box. I came up with nothing, but Blaise found a cracked leather tube that was tagged with a card that said, "This telescope was found at the edge of a clearing near the abandoned home of Jack Finn. November 26, 1922. It is presumed to be the murder weapon in the David Douglas case."

Blaise unscrewed the top of the tube and slid out the telescope. It was dented and crusted with mud. "Maybe this is the proof we're supposed to find?"

"All it proves is that Douglas was killed with it. Why would they think Finn did it?"

"They would if you planted it in his house," Blaise said.

"Oh, sure. I'll walk right past him while he's tossing Douglas's body in the pit and put it on his kitchen table."

"What about after that?"

"You mean when he's coming after me?" I slid the telescope back into the tube.

I was about to give up when I read a *Hilo Tribune* newspaper from 1886. A rusted paperclip held a note on it: "Page 6. Witness to Doctor Douglas Murder Comes Forward."

"The article said that a hunter named Makana told a

reporter that his father saw Finn murder Douglas. He said when his father was on his deathbed, he told the story.

I kept reading, "The boy's father was afraid to say anything because Finn was his boss, and if Finn fired him, he'd have no way to provide for his family. But after Finn moved to Honolulu, he told the sheriff, but Governor Kuakini told the sheriff to ignore it."

Blaise looked at me. "So, who's his father?"

"A guy named Palani."

"Did you meet him when you were back there?"

"Maybe he was there, but I didn't meet him."

"We've got to find him," Blaise said.

"We?"

"Yeah. We've got to both go back together."

"You tried going to the past. It didn't work. Remember?"

"I tried to go back by myself. What if we hold hands and you put on the pouch? Then we go back together, and we take the newspaper and the telescope back with us."

"Then what?"

"You distract Finn, then when he runs after you, I put the telescope in his house right where the other hunters can find it."

"And Finn kills me," I said.

"Lopaka can help you." But I was beginning to wonder if Lopaka would help me. Maybe there was something to Finn's story?

"If we lock arms and then you put on the pouch, guaranteed, it'll work." Blaise rolled up the newspaper and shoved it down his shirt.

"I don't know."

"Come on, cuz. Maybe Papa wants us to do this together."

I was thinking Papa would have been better off if Blaise was at the dump that night. He wouldn't be afraid to travel to the past.

"Let's try."

I held Blaise's hand and I put on the pouch slowly, not

really wanting to do it.

"Don't let go," I said, but I felt Blaise's hand slipping away.

"Noah! Hold on to me!" Blaise yelled.

"I'm trying!" But I was pulled into the past without him.

CHAPTER FOURTEEN

I was back in the same cave where Lopaka left me. It took a minute for my eyes to adjust to the dark. It was all like I left it except Papa wasn't there, Lopaka was.

"Did you find Kia Manu?" I asked.

"Another bird catcher told me she went to Hilo. That's where we planned to meet, so I came back for you. What about you? Did you find anything?"

"My cousin and I found the telescope that Finn killed Douglas with." I held it up.

"Found it? It's already here."

"But it had a note on it that said it was found in a clearing near Finn's house sixty years from now." But the note didn't travel to the past; neither did the newspaper that Blaise tucked under his shirt.

"You made things worse! Now we'll be found with the gold and the murder weapon!"

"We found a witness to the murder." I tried to calm him. "It was in the newspaper forty-two years from now. His name is Palani. Do you know him?"

"Of course," Lopaka said.

"When Palani was on his deathbed, he told his son that he saw Finn kill Douglas, but he made his son promise not to tell anyone because he was afraid of what Finn would do to his family."

Lopaka said, "Everybody's afraid of Finn, even the other hunters."

"Once Finn left the island, Palani's son told the newspaper. So, all we have to do now is to get Palani to admit what he saw."

"Noah, don't you listen? No one is going to accuse Finn of anything."

"What if we put the gold back in Douglas's backpack? Then when the hunters find us, you won't have any gold, and there won't be any reason to accuse you of killing him."

"How are we going to do that? The hunters are at the pit now, pulling up the bull."

"If they're busy with the bull, they won't see us. I can sneak the gold back in Douglas's knapsack, then plant the telescope in his house."

"They'll capture us both, and you'll have the telescope and I'll have the gold."

"I have to try." It was my last chance. I grabbed the telescope. "I'm going."

Lopaka stepped in front of me. "You'll fail."

"Give me the gold."

And Lopaka gave it to me and stepped aside for me to pass.

I headed down the trail, knowing the odds of my plan working weren't great. The farther I went, the more the path narrowed and the slower I went. You've got to do this, I told myself.

Lopaka caught up to me. "Noah, you won't make it alone. If there's any chance for this working, we've got to do it together."

With Lopaka with me, I thought we had a shot.

We made it down the path and squatted in the brush at the edge of the clearing. The hunters were leaning over their ropes. One of them called, "Heave on three." They grabbed the rope tighter. "One, two, . . ."

On "two," Lopaka tackled me and snatched the gold. The pouch ripped and coins spilled out. "Go back to the cave," he yelled.

I picked up the coins and watched him make it to the clearing.

When a hunter yelled, "Pull! Now!" Lopaka ran into the clearing. He was halfway to Douglas's stuff when Finn pointed to him! "There's the guide!"

Lopaka ran back into the woods.

"I'm coming for you, boy!" Finn yelled.

Lopaka grabbed my arm and pulled me. "Run!"

"I hear you, Lopaka." Finn was getting closer.

"Noah, keep up!"

I couldn't go faster. I tried to run, but my chest was bursting. "I can't." I stopped and bent over.

"Do not stop, Noah! You can do this!"

Finn called out to Lopaka again.

"Come on, Noah."

I got to my feet, took a few steps, and my foot caught in a tree root. I fell forward—knees, chest, face—and I heard a crack and felt a bolt of pain shoot from my ankle.

"I'm sure it's broken," I told Lopaka. "Go on without me."

When Lopaka tried to wrench my shoe out of the root, the pain felt like hot barbed wire. I screamed. "Go! Get out of here!"

"I'm not leaving you." Lopaka worked to get my shoe off.

Finn was coming up the trail. "I can smell your fear, boy."

"Go!" I pushed Lopaka away.

Lopaka yanked my foot loose. "

When I stood up, my leg collapsed. "It's not going to work."

"Get on my back." Lopaka squatted in front of me.

I put my arms around his neck, and he piggybacked me to the top of the trail. I felt like I was going to throw up. "Let me down!"

"The cave's right ahead."

"I'm going to be sick."

He set me down next to a boulder. With my first step on the ground, a shard of stone cut my foot.

"I can hear you, boy." Finn's voice was louder.

"The cave's right there." Lopaka bent down for him to carry me on his back.

It was only a few yards away. "I can walk." Using Lopaka as a crutch, I hobbled along, and Lopaka pulled away the curtain of vines.

I made it.

Lopaka helped me down. Then he ripped off a strip of his trousers and bandaged my ankle. It hurt worse than it did before, but I was safe.

"I'm going back on the trail. I'll lead Finn to a fork in the path. Then I'll circle around until he won't be able to track me."

"Stay with me!" I didn't want to be left behind again.

"I have to lead them away or we're both dead."

"What if Finn finds me?"

"Don't move and don't make a sound."

Lopaka left and I was alone.

I heard Finn calling. His voice got louder. I heard twigs snap. Finn was close.

I dragged myself to the entrance and lay flat on my belly, so he wouldn't see me.

I could hear him wheeze. I saw his feet. He stopped in front of the cave, bent over, and put his hands on his knees. "Lopaka! I'm right behind you, boy." Finn caught his breath, then headed up the trail.

He didn't see me.

Then I heard other men coming, maybe three or four. I pulled back the vine just enough to see Charles Harrison leading them.

I thought about calling out to him. In Hilo, Harrison sounded like he thought it was Finn who killed Douglas. I was sure he'd believe us. I was about to call out when I heard Finn's voice, "I got Lopaka."

Finn and Lopaka stumbled down the trail. Lopaka's wrists were tied together, and Finn was jabbing him with his rifle. Finn shoved Lopaka next to the boulder.

"Untie the boy. He can't walk like that," Harrison told Finn.

I watched Finn untie the rope. It fell to the ground, and I heard Finn grunt as he leaned down to pick it up.

Then Finn stopped. He stared at the ground and pawed at the dirt with his hand, then he smelled his fingers and said, "Blood."

It was my blood, and my bloody footprints leading straight to the cave.

CHAPTER FIFTEEN

Finn pulled back the vines. "Look what we have here."

I was done for.

I clawed the wall to get to my feet and hopped on one leg. Lopaka stepped forward to help me.

"Well, there we have it, Harrison." Finn laughed. "Two murdering thieves!"

"I saw you. You killed Douglas!" Tears. Pain shot up my leg.

Finn lifted the pouch from Lopaka's waist. I knew once he saw Douglas's gold, it would be over for us.

"Take it off," Finn told Lopaka.

When Finn emptied the gold coins into his hand, he looked at Harrison. "Told you."

The other hunters in the party stepped closer to see the gold.

"And you," Finn said to me, "empty your pockets."

I remembered the gold coins I picked up when Lopaka dropped them. I had six pieces of gold and there was no use trying to explain.

"Let any doubt be extinguished," Finn said it like he was an actor on stage. I almost expected him to bow.

"We can take them to Hilo." Harrison stared at my foot. "But he needs to be splinted."

Using Lopaka as my crutch, I got down the trail to the

clearing where we caught up to the rest of the hunting party. They all had ideas about how to get me to Hilo. One hunter suggested they carry me in the same sling with the bull's severed head. But another said the bundle would be too heavy for the canvas to hold both me and the head.

In the end, they put one of Douglas's boots on me and tied a rope around the ankle for support. It didn't help with the pain, but it kept my foot off the gravel.

When the hunting party formed up, they marched in the same order I remembered from my first visit to the past when I was marching up the hill. The men carrying the bull's head were first; the men hauling Douglas's gear were second, then the hunters, then Lopaka, me, Charles Harrison, and Jack Finn. I knew one of these men had to be Palani.

We walked for an hour. The rain that started as a slight drizzle became a dousing rain and I could only see a few feet in front of me.

When we got to a stream, the men stopped. The hunters yelled back and forth to each other, but their voices were drowned out by the downpour.

I asked Lopaka what they were saying. He shouted over the rain, but the only words I could make out were, "flash flood," "cross now," "wait it out."

I had seen one flash flood in my life. I was on a Boy Scout trip on Kauai. A small stream went from a trickle to a three-foot surge in seconds.

The men argued. Harrison said we should go. Finn wanted to wait. I couldn't believe I was siding with Finn. In the end, Harrison convinced them and waved the party forward.

The first men to cross were the men carrying Douglas's things, the second had the bull. Between the first and second groups, the stream went from ankle-deep to knee-deep.

At first, the sling with the bull in it dangled over the stream, but by the time they crossed, the water had risen so high that it was a foot underwater.

I looked upstream but didn't see any rise. I hoped it reached its peak.

Lopaka and I were next. Charles Harrison and Finn were last.

"Hang on," Lopaka said, and I got on his back.

My feet dangled in the water, then in seconds it was at my knees. We were halfway across when I saw the surge coming.

"Look out," Harrison yelled.

The water hit us. I tumbled off Lopaka's back.

"Turn back!" Finn screamed.

It felt like a water hose.

Lopaka yelled, "Swim to me."

I was upside down. I kicked up, and my head popped out of the water.

"Noah." Lopaka reached for me.

I was sucked under again. I flailed, gulping for air.

Up. I've got to swim up.

I felt a hand reach for me.

I was under again. My lungs burned and I couldn't see which way was up.

My hands hit the bottom and I kept swirling.

I was going to die.

I felt someone's arms around me and locked on to his neck.

My arms slipped, but he lifted me. I was up.

"Hold on."

My hands kept slipping.

"I've got you!"

Men yelled. They passed me from one to another and carried me to shore. They set me on my belly.

"Breathe!" They slapped my back until I choked up water and gulped the air.

I was alive. The rain beat on my face, and the wind sliced into my skin, but I was alive.

"Live, boy!" It was Papa's voice.

When I woke the next morning, I was curled under an *ohia*

tree, covered with a *tapa* blanket. The sun was up, the rain was gone, and the wind had died down.

Charles Harrison approached. "How are you?"

"Fine."

"We weren't sure you were going to make it through the night. Lopaka kept you dry and kept believing you would live."

I smiled.

"I don't think you would have pulled through without him."

I was sent to save Lopaka's life, but he saved mine.

Harrison waved over an older man with white hair and a long, white beard. Harrison said something in Hawaiian to him, and the man walked away. When he came back, the man was carrying a bundle of ti leaves.

He laid the leaves down in a row, then kneeled next to me. As he stripped the veins from the leaves, he said, "I'm Palani."

Palani! "You saw Finn kill Doctor Douglas."

He stared at me and went back to stripping the leaves.

I grabbed his arm. "I know you saw him. You've got to tell Reverend Newhouse."

He didn't stop working.

"You know Lopaka and I are innocent!"

Palani braided the leaves into a sandal.

"I'm begging you," I said. "You're the only one who can save us."

"I saw nothing."

"If you don't, we'll both hang."

Palani shaped and twisted the leaves into a boot and fitted it to my foot.

"Why won't you say anything? We'll die if you don't?"

"I work for Mr. Finn."

"We can take care of you," I said. "Reverend Newhouse, Lopaka, me."

He tied the boot to my foot. "This will hold until we get to Hilo." He stood up and walked away.

84

There went my last hope.

When Lopaka was finished helping break camp, he came and sat next to me.

"Palani won't help us," I said.

"He can't," Lopaka said.

"He's got to!"

"Noah, you still don't understand."

He was right. How could a man let two boys be hanged for a murder they didn't commit?

"Come with me." He helped me stand and we walked toward the bank of the stream to a cove where I saw Papa.

"Noah!" He held me. "My Noah."

I heard him sob.

Papa stepped back and looked at my foot.

"I'm OK," I said.

He held my shoulders. "Noah, can you ever forgive me? I should have made the Night Marcher take me."

"I know what happened now, Papa. It was my fault. You pushed my face down. I'm the one who had to look."

"No!" Papa insisted. "I should have taught you the old ways."

"And I should have listened to you when you told me to keep my head down."

"You've done the best you could," Papa said. "We almost lost you, again." Papa took a deep breath. "It's time for you to go home. You've come back three times. You almost died, there's nothing more you can do."

"I'm not done."

"Noah, listen to him," Lopaka said. "We're both sending you home,"

"What will happen if I go?"

"Kia Manu will help me."

"And you, Papa. If I go home, will your spirit ever rest?"

"I'm at peace with whatever happens," Papa said. "Give me the pouch."

I heard a bird call and looked up. "Did you hear that? Maybe it's Kia Manu?"

"It doesn't matter," Lopaka said.

"The pouch, Noah," Papa held out his hand.

I turned to Lopaka. "Call out to Kia Manu! Talk to her!"

Lopaka answered, "Whatever happens, is meant to be."

"Give me the pouch, Noah."

"If I do, how can I come back?"

"You can't." Papa shook his head.

"Go home, Noah. Enjoy your life and think of me." He smiled.

"I love you, Papa."

I handed the pouch to him.

CHAPTER SIXTEEN

When I came back to my own time, Blaise was waiting for me at Lopaka's grave, and I was still crying.

"You OK?" Blaise said.

I wiped my tears with my shirt. "Papa sent me home. So did Lopaka. They released me."

"So, it's over?"

"Nothing's changed. Lopaka will hang."

"What about Papa?" Blaise asked.

"He wouldn't say it, but I don't think his spirit will rest."

"You've got to go back."

"I can't. Papa took the pouch."

Blaise stared at the ground. "There's another way," he said. "We can talk to Uncle Solomon."

"This is way beyond Uncle Solomon," I said.

"No, you'll see." Blaise got out his phone.

"Don't text him," I said.

"Noah, you promised you'd talk to him."

Blaise texted Uncle Solomon that we'd be at the firehouse in twenty minutes.

"He knows the old ways. You got to tell him the whole story."

"You want me to tell him I time traveled, and I saw Papa?"

"He'll believe you."

I knew it wouldn't work, but I promised Blaise. "OK," I said, knowing this was going to end up in a disaster.

Blaise helped me up. My foot still hurt. I leaned against Lopaka's stone, and I watched the words on it change. His name was still there, but the rest of the words were fading, and two new words appeared: "convicted" and "murderer."

I pointed to the words.

"We got to talk to Uncle Solomon right away," Blaise said.

We biked to the firehouse. A long, white tent was set up for food prep for the chili fest. Rows of cafeteria tables were lined end-to-end with firefighters and their families, working in an assembly line of rinsing, chopping, shredding, and peeling food.

At card tables, little kids wrapped forks and knives into napkins. And outside the tent on the grass, high school kids painted signs: "Chili Fest Fundraiser, $15.00, Memorial Day. 9 a.m. until we sell out."

Uncle Solomon was chopping beef into cubes.

"So, what's up, boys?" Uncle kept chopping.

Blaise looked around. "We need to talk in private."

"Oh, yeah? It must be important." He laughed.

"It's about Papa," I said.

"Papa's in trouble," Blaise said.

"Papa?" Uncle's face was serious.

"He's in big trouble," Blaise said. "And so is Noah."

Uncle Solomon didn't act like we were joking. He set down his knife and pulled off his gloves. "Let's talk in my truck."

Uncle's truck was a '51 Dodge pickup with a rusted floorboard and a piece of plywood covering the holes.

He pulled down the tailgate, and Blaise and I hopped up on it. "Talk to me," he said.

Blaise blurted out, "Noah had a dream about the Kekoa curse, and it came true."

"Did you know the story of the Kekoa curse?" I asked him.

"Yeah, but I thought it was one of your grandmother's tales."

"It's not," I said, and I told him everything that happened, right up to Papa taking the pouch away from me.

Uncle Solomon covered his mouth with his hand and paced back and forth. "Noah, you made the promise to the Night Marcher? Not to Lopaka?"

"Yes."

"And it was you, not Papa, who made the promise?"

I nodded.

"Do you remember the exact words you promised?"

"I was four. I don't even remember doing it."

Uncle took my hand in his and ran his thumb over the Night Marcher's mark. "Then it's the Night Marcher who has to release you, not Lopaka or your Papa."

"How?"

"We go to the Pali, and you ask him."

"You want me to talk to a Night Marcher?" I knew we shouldn't have told Uncle Solomon. "Just looking at a Night Marcher got me into this mess."

"It's the only way."

I broke down in tears. It was all too much. The past. Finn. Failing. Lopaka was going to hang, and Papa would never be at peace.

Uncle helped me down from the tailgate. "We are *ohana*. We can do this together."

I was desperate to find a way. I didn't have any hope he could fix it, but I got in the truck with Blaise wedged next to the stick shift and me pressed against the passenger door.

"Where did you see the Marchers?" Uncle asked.

I told him everything I remembered.

"Then we go there and wait."

"What if they don't come?"

"They'll come."

"How will I know which one he is?"

"He'll know you."

"And then?"

"You talk to him."

We drove out of town, onto the Old Pali Road where the banyan tree roots hung so low they touched the ground.

When we turned onto Dump Road, Uncle asked me where Papa parked that night.

"I don't remember."

"Think, Noah. Was there a tree where you parked? Did the road curve? Was there a stream nearby? Close your eyes and remember."

I closed my eyes and all I saw was dark. "I think there was a duck pond."

Blaise said, "There's a pond right after this curve."

"That's where we start," Uncle said.

"And there was a path that led to the pond," I said.

Uncle Solomon pulled over and parked behind a duct-taped refrigerator on the side of the road.

I looked out the window. "This looks right."

We got out of the truck.

"Where did you go from here?" Uncle asked.

"Papa was looking for a Volkswagen hubcap. He couldn't find one, so we had to walk deeper into the valley."

"Then we keep walking," Uncle Solomon said.

The deeper we walked into the woods, the darker it got. At first, I didn't recognize anything, it all looked alike—giant monstera, palm trees, scrub brush—then I stopped. I didn't see anything different; it was how I felt. It was the way the wind blew down the valley.

"It was here," I said.

"Good," Uncle said, and he told me we would wait there for them. "When they come, you stand to greet him. Blaise and I will lie flat on the ground and cover our eyes."

I thought this was never going to work, but we all waited and waited and waited.

"What if he doesn't come?" I asked.

"Patience."

Blaise and Uncle were cross-legged on the ground when the wind gusted, and the air smelled of rot.

"Get down!" Uncle ordered Blaise, and the two of them lay face down and covered their heads with their hands.

The marchers were coming. The drums. The chant. I stood tall.

Then one stepped in front of me and shouted, "Naʻu." He is mine. And the rest kept marching.

I looked at the Night Marcher. My heart pounded. "I'm here to ask you to release me from my promise."

His eyes glowed orange. "You want me to release you?"

"No," I stuttered. "I want to go back."

"You have been back, and you failed."

"I want to make things *pono*," I said. "I have to save Lopaka, but I can't, my Papa took the pouch."

"How will you keep your promise?" The Night Marcher's breath smelled like sulfur.

"I'll do anything," I said. "You tell me how."

"It's your *kuleana*, not mine!" The air thundered.

"I don't know the old ways," I started to bargain with him. "I need you to teach me."

The ground rumbled.

"I'll do anything. Teach me," I said.

"If you fail, you will die," he said.

I begged him, "I love my Papa, it was me who looked at you, not him. Spare him. Send me back even if I die."

"It's done," he said, and the air thundered.

CHAPTER SEVENTEEN

I was back in Hilo. It was the middle of the night, and I was sitting on the ground in the hale where the bull and Douglas's body were brought. My ankles and wrists were tied and, around my waist was a rope that tethered me to a leg of the table.

When I looked around for Lopaka, a hand clamped over my mouth.

Finn whispered in my ear, "It's just the two of us now. And soon, it'll be just you."

I tried to shake myself free.

"I'm going to let go of you, and you are going to keep your mouth shut. Understand?"

I nodded, and he let go of my mouth.

"Where's Lopaka?" I asked.

"Gone. Just like I warned you. He's gone and you're going to hang."

I screamed, "Help!"

Finn clamped my mouth tighter. "You don't listen so good, boy. I told you to shut up."

We were face-to-face. "This is my last warning. Understand? If you scream, I'll put my knife through you."

I nodded.

He let go and reached for a neckerchief out of his pocket. I looked around for anything I could use as a weapon, but there was nothing.

"Open your mouth." He twisted the neckerchief tight.

"First, tell me where Lopaka is."

"He abandoned you. I told you he would."

"Lopaka wouldn't do that."

"Oh, but he did." Finn laughed.

I thought if I kept him talking, maybe Reverend Newhouse would hear us. "Tell me why you killed Douglas."

"I didn't plan on it. I was just going to rob him. Then he tried to kill me. I had to save myself," he snarked.

"You bashed his head in, then you sat there and laughed!"

"It was self-defense." Finn forced the gag into my mouth.

"Liar!" I screamed as loud as I could, but Finn pulled the cloth so tight, I

gasped for air.

"Listen, my little friend," Finn said. "There's a ship leaving for Tahiti on the morning tide, and I got myself signed on the crew." He yanked the neckerchief even tighter. "I'll be long gone on the sea before the good reverend gets out of bed." He stood. "Give the reverend a message from me. You tell him I never intended to kill the doctor. You got that? It was self-defense. And you, you don't learn." He smacked the back of my head. "I kept telling you to stay out of things that don't concern you." Then, he ran his finger over the rim of his hat and walked away.

When I was sure he was out of earshot, I screamed for help, but my yelling sounded like a muffled gurgle.

I stamped my feet and kicked over a bucket, but no one heard me. There was no sign of

life in the reverend's house.

The stars were still out, and the moon cast a blue light. It would be hours before the reverend woke.

I slid my jaw back and forth, trying to loosen the gag. That just made the corners of my lips bleed. I rubbed my wrists against each other, hoping it would loosen the ropes, but it was useless. All I could do was wait.

Maybe the reverend would wake up in time to stop Finn? He had to believe Finn was the murderer.

All the reverend had to do was wake up.

I waited. Fleas swarmed around me and landed on my lips where they were bleeding.

I waited some more.

The sky went from black to gray, but there was still no sign of life in the house. I saw a figure approach. Could it be Papa?

But it was Lopaka who stepped out of the night shadows. He was with a Hawaiian woman I guessed to be Kia Manu.

"What are you doing here?" Lopaka asked me.

I raised my face to him to show him the gag.

As he untied the gag, Lopaka asked, "How did you come back without the pouch?"

Noah shrugged off the gag and said, "Finn's gone! He signed on a ship." I looked at the woman. She had long dark hair and the muscles in her arms were shadowed by the moonlight. "Are you Kia Manu?"

"I am."

"Finn escaped," I said. "We need to wake Reverend Newhouse."

"I'll go," Kia Manu said, and Lopaka nodded as he untied the ropes on my wrists and ankles.

"Why did you come back to Hilo?" I asked Lopaka. "I thought Kia Manu was taking you to a sanctuary."

"We decided to come back so Kia Manu could tell Reverend Newhouse what she saw. We knew he'd believe her." Lopaka untangled the rope at my waist. "When did Finn leave?"

"Maybe an hour ago? I can't tell," I said. "It was still dark."

"Do you know the name of his ship?"

"I know it's headed for Tahiti and it's sailing this morning." I stood up and brushed the gravel from my trousers.

"We've got to stop him."

"We have to wait for Reverend Newhouse."

"I can't wait." I started to run.

Lopaka grabbed my arm. "We need the reverend with us."

I broke loose and ran.

Lopaka shouted, "No one will believe you!"

"I've got to try."

I ran down past the sailmaker's shop, the blacksmith's, down to the harbor where there were dozens of ships, but only four were docked at the pier, and only one of those was getting ready to sail. Its gangway was clogged with men pushing carts, carrying canvas, and leading goats onto the deck. I made it to the pier when Lopaka caught up. He grabbed my arm and yanked it behind my back.

"You're hurting me!"

"I told you. We have to wait for Reverend Newhouse. He's with Kia Manu now, they're on their way."

I spotted a man on deck wearing a red coat and a black top hat. I was sure he was the captain. I yelled up to him, "You have a murderer on board."

"Noah, you're making things worse!"

The captain looked down.

I yelled up to him. "Jack Finn's a murderer. He killed Doctor Douglas. I have proof."

Lopaka held me back.

"Captain, please. Listen to me!"

The captain waved at the men on the gangway. "Let him pass," he said, and Lopaka let go of me and they let me pass.

When I got on board, I looked at all the men on the dock, but I didn't see Finn.

"It's Jack Finn, the bull hunter," I told the captain. "He's a murderer. He's here somewhere."

"I'm right here." Finn stepped out from the crowd. "The boy's lost his mind."

It felt like every man on deck stopped what he was doing

and looked at me.

"Who are you, boy?" the captain asked.

"It's not important who I am," I said. "It's him." I pointed to Finn. "He's a murderer."

The captain walked toward us. "Finn, what do you say to all of this?"

"Captain, you know me." Finn's voice was smooth. "This boy's trying to save his own skin. It was him and his native friend who murdered the doctor."

The captain ordered, "Bring me the native boy," and two men grabbed Lopaka by the

elbows and pushed him up the gangway.

"Captain," Lopaka said, "Reverend Newhouse is coming with a witness who will tell you that Finn killed the doctor."

"And who would that be?" Finn demanded.

"Kia Manu," Lopaka said.

Finn threw his head back, laughing. "A bird catcher?" He turned to the captain. "Are you going to take the word of a bird catcher over mine?"

"Kia Manu is a bird catcher for the king," Lopaka said. "He trusts her."

"Who are you?" the captain asked Lopaka.

"Lopaka Aiona. I was Douglas's guide."

Reverend Newhouse and Kia Manu were running to the pier. "Reverend Newhouse is here," I said. "They're coming. Look!"

"Let them pass," the captain said, and Reverend Newhouse and Kia Manu boarded the ship.

Reverend Newhouse greeted the captain. "Captain." He bowed his head.

"Reverend." The captain bowed back.

"You know I am loath to engage in matters of the law, but in this case, I must come forward. There are three witnesses to the murder of Doctor Douglas. This woman who is a bird catcher for the king." He motioned to Kia Manu. "Lopaka

Aiona, a trusted guide, and this boy, a visitor to our island."

Kia Manu stepped forward. She stood tall with her chin up and her eyes on Finn. "Captain, this man killed Doctor Douglas. He beat him beyond what any man would do to an animal, then he shoved his body into a pit with a trapped bull."

"Fools' tales." Finn scoffed. "Ask Reverend Newhouse. These boys had Douglas's gold on them when they were caught."

"It's true," Reverend Newhouse said. "Both boys had gold."

"And I had none!" Finn said.

"I saw you, Finn," Kia Manu said, "I watched you scavenge his body."

I remembered Finn emptying Douglas's boots, digging through his pockets. I remembered the ring! He must still have it!

"Captain, Finn has the doctor's gold ring," I said. "He cut off the doctor's finger to get it."

"The boy's mad," Finn said.

"With respect, captain. Have your men search him," Kia Manu said, and the captain ordered it.

Two sailors stepped toward Finn. As soon as they did, Finn grabbed the first one and put a knife to the sailor's throat. "Listen to me, captain," Finn said. "I did kill Douglas, but it was self-defense."

"Let the sailor go, Finn," the captain demanded.

"Ask anyone of them who saw it. Douglas came at me with a knife. Isn't that true, boy?" He looked at me. "He was going to kill me."

"You sidestepped him, and the doctor fell, then you bludgeoned him," I said.

"He attacked me!"

"You killed him and chopped off his finger."

Kia Manu walked toward Finn. "You cut off his finger to steal his ring."

"Step back, old woman," Finn warned.

But she kept walking slowly, speaking softly as she did, "And it's that ring that's going to condemn you!"

Finn still had a knife to the sailor's throat.

"Give me the knife." Kia Manu was inches from him. "The knife, Finn." She put her hand out.

Finn didn't move.

"The knife." Kia Manu's eyes never left Finn's.

"Do as she says, Finn," the captain said.

As soon as Finn handed it to her, sailors surrounded him.

"Show us the ring," the captain said.

"Tell your sailors to let go of me, and I'll show you." He shrugged off the sailors. He dug deep in his pocket and held it up.

The captain examined the ring. "The initials are *DD*. David Douglas."

Finn protested. "Douglas came after me with a knife."

"He was a small man," I said. "You didn't have to kill him. You could have taken him!"

Reverend Newhouse said, "Captain, you have three witnesses to the murder."

"Yes," The captain said, "but I have no rights here. I have to turn Finn over to Governor Kuakini."

"No!" I shouted. "You can't."

Reverend Newhouse put his hand on my shoulder, then he said to the captain, "May I point out that both Douglas and Finn are British citizens? That would make this crime and any judgment of it a matter for the British consul."

"I left Britain when I was a boy," Finn said. "I live here. And Kuakini is my governor."

The captain said, "Reverend Newhouse is correct. You are a British citizen, as is Doctor Douglas. So, I'm obliged to deliver you to the British consul in Honolulu."

"You will regret this, captain!" Finn threatened. "Kuakini will punish you for this. He will forbid your ship ever to dock in Hilo!"

"Take him below," the captain told the sailors.

Finn was still shouting as they led him away.

Finn was to be handed over to the British consul. It was over. Lopaka was free and I had fulfilled my *kuleana*.

I looked at Reverend Newhouse, at Kia Manu, and Lopaka, knowing I would never return

to the past again.

"You saved my life," Lopaka said.

"We all did," I said. "My cousin, Reverend Newhouse, Kia Manu, you. We all did it."

Lopaka hugged me, and when he did, I spotted Papa on the dock.

"I love you," I mouthed to him.

Aloha au iā ʻoe. Papa kissed his hand and waved it at me.

CHAPTER EIGHTEEN

Blaise and I biked through the cemetery a lot that summer. Sometimes we'd stop by Lopaka's grave and read the inscription: "Here lies Lopaka Aiona. Born 1820. Died 1888. Husband. Father. Guide to us all."

We'd pick up some rubbish, pull a few weeds, and tell Lopaka what was going on with us. And if Mr. Goodall was around, Blaise would talk to him about our plan to make a video for next year's History Day even though we both knew we never would.

It was the last week of summer when Blaise and I were walking home from playing basketball and we stopped by and visited Lopaka. It had been over a week since we were there, and we knew there'd be rubbish. But that day, there was more than rubbish. Leaning against Lopaka's stone was a Volkswagen hubcap.

Blaise and I looked at each other.

"Do you think Papa left it?" he asked.

"Got to be," I said.

Blaise ran his hand over the hubcap. "There's some rust and a few dents, but it's in good shape. We could make a video about it for History Day."

"Or maybe not," I said.

Blaise ran his hand over the hubcap. "There's some rust

and a few dents, but it's in good shape."

"It's a classic." I eyed the empty Safeway cart next to the maintenance shed. "I bet Mr. Goodall wouldn't mind if we borrowed it."

We high-fived each other.

We lifted the hubcap into the shopping cart. Each of us had one hand on the cart and one on our treasure. The cart rattled and shook, and Blaise and I made loud beeping noises for pedestrians to step aside for us because we were taking home the most special, dented, and rusted VW hubcap that anyone could ever find.

AUTHOR'S NOTE: QUESTIONS & ANSWERS

Are the Night Marchers real?

Tales of *Huaka'i Pō* (Night Marchers) are strongly woven into old Hawaiian culture. And every time the stories are told, the warning is given: Do not look at a Night Marcher, or you will die.

The first written story about the Night Marchers is in a register from when Captain Cook arrived on the islands in the 1770s. (About the same time as the American Revolutionary War.) Before the English and Americans came to Hawai'i, there was no written language. Hawai'i had an oral tradition. That means the history of the people was passed down in story, chant, and myth.

That first written observation describes a *huaka'i* (a procession) of *oi'o* ("spirit ranks") led by the spirit of King Kamehameha, who was pacing angrily on the Big Island of Hawai'i.

Both then and in modern times, witnesses describe a foul-smelling wind, *oli* (chanting), *pū* (conch-shell blowing), and a procession of bright torches before the Night Marchers arrive.

Nanette Napoleon Purnell, a local historian of Hawai'i, told me that kind of procession was common in ancient times. *Ali'i* (chiefs) would visit different villages to collect "taxes," visit their people and their land, or travel to their summer palaces.

Lopaka Kapanui, a Hawaiian cultural storyteller, says the

kindest chiefs would travel at night because looking at a chief was a *kapu* (taboo), and if broken, resulted in death. Commoners were expected to lie on the ground and stare at the earth to avoid accidentally looking at the *ali'i*.

Some stories say the commoner should take off all his clothes and slather his body with mud, so the Night Marcher would not smell his presence.

According to *Kaulana Mahina* (Hawaiian Moon Calendar) there are certain dates the Night Marchers appear more often. *Po Kane*, the twenty-seventh day of the moon cycle, is a favorite. Another favorite night is the *Po Akua*, the fourteenth night of the new moon.

There are also places where Night Marchers are seen most often. On Oahu, where I live, those places include the Nu'uanu Pali. In the story of *Past Whispers*, Noah sees the Night Marchers at the foot of the Pali on Dump Road.

Some witnesses say they hear the pounding of footsteps and see footprints of the Marchers on their path, but others say the Marchers float a few inches off the ground. However, they all agree on a foul smell, like sulfur, and seeing lines of torches come down from the mountains, but not all agree about the beating of the *pahu* (drums).

Nannette Purnell reminded me that the Night Marchers are not evil, they are simply doing their job to protect the *ali'i*. That was their job during life, and it continues after death. So, you never see a Night Marcher alone. They travel as warrior-protectors, often six across, three women and three men.

Lopaka Kapanui explains that if a commoner looks at a Night Marcher, no matter what the reason—by accident, or too much courage or curiosity—he will hear a shriek of *o'ia* which means, "Let him be pierced," and that'll be the end of you!

But if a Night Marcher recognizes you, he will shout, *na'u* (mine) and the commoner will be saved.

Today, there are tours in Honolulu that include stories of

Night Marchers. There is a sense of reverence and fear in people who have seen the Night Marchers. And there is also a sense of pride because it is believed that only people who can see or hear wonder and fear and have a "right heart" can see them.

So, are the Night Marchers real? You decide, but if, by chance, you ever encounter one, you know what to do.

How did David Douglas really die?

The first time I heard about David Douglas's death, I was on a family vacation on the Big island. I read an article in the *Coffee Times* by Betty Leo-Fullard about it, and I was hooked. I researched Douglas's death for many years. I had the facts, but I didn't have a story until I was having lunch with my grandsons at Kualoa Ranch. I told them the facts, and together we wove a story. *Forgotten Oath* is a story.

The characters are made up, and so are all their conversations. The characters may have been inspired by real-life people, but the people on the page are figments of my imagination. Even the town of Hilo that I describe is what Hilo looked like in the 1890s, not in 1834.

What do we know for a fact?

We know that in July 1834, David Douglas started on a hike from Kona to Hilo on the Big Island, but he never got to Hilo. And we know that his body was found in a pit used to trap bulls by Hawaiian men who worked for Ned Gurney. (And, yes, there really was a live bull in it!)

Ned Gurney was born in London in 1800. His family was poor, and Ned stole to support them. He was caught twice stealing copper from the roof of a building. The second time he was caught, he was sentenced to seven years of hard labor at Botany Bay Penal Colony in Australia.

Many of the men sent to Botany Bay were young (Ned was nineteen when he was sent) and were used as laborers for

British building projects, including building warships.

When he was at Botany Bay, Ned helped build the war-ship, *Prince Regent*. The *Regent* was a gift from King George IV to King Kamehameha II (Liholiho).

When it was finished, the British ship, *Mermaid*, accompanied the *Prince Regent* to Hawai'i. The crew of the *Regent* was supposed to sail back to Australia on it. When the *Mermaid* docked in Honolulu, three prisoners jumped ship. Ned Gurney was one of them.

According to legend, Ned escaped to the Big Island where he married, had a child, and became a bullock hunter. He was such an outstanding hunter that he became one of Governor Kuakini's favorites. Although the governor favored Ned, not everyone did. Many missionaries and other bullock hunters thought he wasn't to be trusted, and a missionary's wife wrote in her diary that Gurney was a "rough man" and "the world would be a better place without him."

What else is true?

Douglas's body was removed from the pit and taken to Hilo where it was examined, but the men who examined it came to no conclusion about how he died. So, they shipped the body to Honolulu where medical doctors could discover the cause of death. (The words used by the character Mr. Wilcocks when he observes Douglas's body are true. But Mr. Wilcocks is a figment of my imagination.)

By the time the people on the Big Island found a ship that would take the body to Honolulu, weeks went by, and Douglas's body deteriorated so badly that when it arrived in Honolulu, the doctors who examined it could not determine a cause of death.

How did Douglas die?

Some historians think Douglas was murdered by Edward "Ned" Gurney. Some think he accidentally slipped into the pit because his eyesight was so poor. And there are a few who think he committed suicide.

My opinion is that Ned Gurney killed him.

But what if Gurney didn't kill Douglas? What if Douglas accidentally fell into the pit?

The facts are that Douglas's campsite was forty feet from the bullock trap and his dog Billie was tied to a post.

Douglas had seen many of these traps before and would have known it was dangerous to get too close. But let's say he was curious and wanted to see the bull. Could he have fallen into the pit? Could it be he didn't see the edge clearly?

Douglas had poor eyesight. In 1828, he fell into a mountain crevasse while he was hiking in Oregon, and he was rescued by a trapper. When the trapper asked him how he fell, Douglas said he "misjudged the depth of the ravine" because his eyesight was "poor" from being exposed to "the brilliant snow and the glaring sun."

A year before he died, Douglas wrote in a letter to the British Horticultural Society, "I am blind in my right eye."

And only six months before he died, he wrote in his journal, "I am struck by an inflammation of the eyes" and reported that his guide had to "put a few drops of opium in my eyes for instant relief." (In those days, a liquid form of opium called laudanum was commonly used as medicine.)

Could Douglas's eyesight have been so bad he misjudged the edge of the pit and accidentally fell into it? We don't know.

Then there's the suicide theory.

David Douglas's work was going badly, and he suspected the British Horticultural

Society was going to fire him. Several young explorers working for the British Horticultural Society were on the Big Island when Douglas died. (There are a few people who think those botanists killed Douglas, but that makes no sense. They knew Douglas was losing the respect of the Horticultural Society and they were being given more and better explorations.)

During Douglas's last trip to Canada, he had two accidents. In one, his canoe got caught in the rapids of Fraser River and smashed against a rocky island. All members of his team survived, but Douglas's entire collection of plants (over 400 species) was gone.

Afterward, Douglas wrote a letter to his friend. "This disastrous occurrence has much broken my strength and my spirit." In the second accident, his team got caught in a storm off the coast of Hudson Bay. Their boats sank. They lost most of their instruments, all their food, water, and blankets, and were given up for dead. When the team returned to base camp, they were all sick and weak.

It was right after the second accident that Douglas asked the British Horticultural Society for money to return home to London. In those days, the way to get home would be by taking a ship from the West Coast of the United States to England. But he asked the society if he could go by a route from Alaska through Russia. The society refused and told him to board a ship in San Francisco. The only way to get to San Francisco was to take a ship from Alaska to Honolulu. Then that ship would sail to California.

When the society refused his request, Douglas was sure they were going to fire him when he got home. He knew there were other botanists the society was sending on explorations instead of him. These younger botanists worked in groups and were politically clever. Douglas was fiercely independent, never understood politics, and thought his work should speak for itself.

During his life, Douglas traveled over 12,000 miles on foot, canoe, and sled, collecting and classifying plant specimens. When he brought these back to London, the society cultivated and sold them for a handsome profit.

Some of the historians who believe Douglas committed suicide base their theory on the fact that Douglas was depressed because he knew he would be fired and, because his vision and health were poor, he intentionally fell into the pit.

What happened the day he died?
We know Douglas started a ninety-mile hike from Kona to Hilo in the company of a man named John. John was an African American servant of Reverend Deill. According to legend, John could not keep up with Douglas, so Douglas went on without him.

John was never suspected of murdering Douglas by anyone who lived at that time.

Were there any witnesses to Douglas's death?
Well, maybe. In 1896, sixty-two years after Douglas died, a Hawaiian man named Bolabola told the Hilo newspaper that when he was a boy of ten, he saw Gurney kill Douglas.

Bolabola said, "Douglas was murdered. We all felt so at the time but were afraid to say so and only whispered it among ourselves."

What happened to Douglas's body?
The account of preparing Douglas's body to be shipped to Honolulu is true. After it was shipped to Honolulu, the doctors examined it and concluded it was too decayed to determine the cause of death, and the body was "temporarily" buried in the cemetery of the Kawaiahaʻo Church.

Letters went back and forth between Honolulu and London to decide whether Douglas should be buried in Honolulu or returned to England. By the time a decision was made, twenty years passed. The British decided his body should stay in Honolulu, and in 1854, a headstone from the British Horticultural Society arrived for him. But by that time, no one at the mission knew where his body was buried.

So, the headstone was bolted to the outside wall of the church. After several years of being exposed to the sun, wind, and rain, the headstone was moved inside the church to protect it. If you go into the church, turn right at the main doors, and look into the vestibule next to the stairs leading to the choir loft, you'll see Douglas's headstone bolted to the wall. The stone is so worn down it is almost impossible to read. Even if you could read the letters, the words are in Latin.

The English translation is: "Here lies David Douglas. Born in Scotland in 1799, who being an indefatigable traveler, was sent out by the British Horticultural Society of London and fell victim to science in the wilds of Hawaii on the 12th day of July 1834."

There is another monument to David Douglas on the Big Island near the spot where his body was found. The place is known as *Kalauakauka* which means The Doctor's Pit. The memorial is a small rock monument on a road that can only be accessed by a four-wheel-drive vehicle and is rarely visited.

We probably will never know how David Douglas died, but we can appreciate all he did. He was a brave man who spent his entire life as an explorer and a discoverer who mapped out the frontiers of North America and Hawai'i.

GLOSSARY

Aloha au iā ʻoe
I love you.

Haʻa
The Hawaiian word *haʻa* has its roots in the Māori word *haka*. Traditionally, haka was performed by the Māori to intimidate their enemies in war. However, there are several versions of *haka/haʻa*. In modern times, it can be used as a welcome chant or a chant to honor a special guest or deceased person or to open a ceremony. And some professional and university athletic teams have had their own *haka/haʻa* compow3e.

In *Past Whispers*, the character Noah chants part of the University of Hawaii's *haʻa*. Here the Haʻa, *or Haʻa Koa* (Warrior Dance) is translated in full:

Mokomoko
Kaena . . . Pa
Eia makou na puali koa o Hawaiʻi
Pulu pe i ka ua koko Tuahine
Pali ku o Puʻu Ohiʻa
Ka manamana
O ke au i ka huli, wela ka honua

U ke au i ka huli, lole ka lani
He lua'i ai la, hua'ina ka wa'a kaua
E Ku mehe Ku, e Ku! E Ku!
E Ku nui a kea, e Ku! E Ku!
E Ku lanakila, e Ku! E Ku!
Kulili'aikaua, e Ku! E Ku!
E Ku i ke koa o Hawai'i e

Translation:

Fighting stance
Boast, begin!
Here we are, fearless Hawai'i warriors
Drenched in the red Tuahine rain
Upright cliff of Pu'u Ohi'a
Thrust the appendage
In the time of change, hot was the earth
In the time of change, turned inside-out, the heavens
An eruption occurred, gushed forth the
molten lava of battle
Stand as Ku, spirit of manhood. Stand, stand!
Oh Ku, spirit of the vastly powerful. Oh Ku, oh Ku!
Oh Ku, spirit of victory. Oh Ku, oh Ku!
Oh Ku, spirit of ferocity in battle. Oh Ku, oh Ku!
Stand to the courage of all Hawai'i.

Source: University of Hawaii, *Ka Leo*: https://www.manoanow.org/kaleo/special_issues/the-new-haa/article_04e4e8c0-891f-11e6-98bb-2b009ea4436f.html

Hale
House, building lodge. Some may be open-walled structures or two-story buildings.

Hala tree
Hala is the local term for a pandanus tree. Sometimes it is called

screw pine or screw palm. In Hawai'i they are called false pine-apple because they have a pineapple-like fruit on them. Their roots form a teepee-like pyramid to hold the trunk.

Source: University of Hawaii, College of Tropical Agriculture. http://www2.hawaii.edu/~eherring/hawnprop/pan-tect.htm

Hanau
To give birth.
Happy Birthday is translated into Hawaiian as *Hau'oli Lā Hānau*.

Haole
There are many definitions for this word. The most common current usage is to refer to a Caucasian person. It is sometimes translated as white or without breath. One dictionary says it originally meant a foreigner.

Ipu
A hollowed-out gourd. Sometimes used as a bottle, urn, dish, mug, container, pot, or basin. It is also used as a drum con-sisting of a single gourd or two large gourds of unequal size joined together.

Kia Manu
Bird catchers in ancient Hawai'i were called Kia Manu. It also means the method of catching birds by gumming a stick. The most prized feathers the kia manu collected were from the *mamo* bird and were used to make capes for the Hawaiian roy-alty.

Kapa (Tapa)
The HAWAIIAN DICTIONARY says kapa is tapa made from the mulberry bush bark. It was used for clothes, bedclothes, quilts, and decorations. I chose to use the more common term *tapa* rather than the more traditional term *kapa* because I thought more people would know what it was.

Kuakini

John Adams Kuakini was appointed as the Governor of Hawai'i Island in 1829. He gave land to missionaries and built a low lava wall on the island as a barrier against the bullocks wandering through the villages. This wall was called *Ka pā nui o Kuakini* (The Great Wall of Kuakini) and parts of it still stand today.

Source: The List of Royal Governors of O'ahu Archived at the Hawai'i State Archives

Kuleana

The Hawaiian word *kuleana* carries many cultural meanings, including: right, privilege, concern, responsibility, business, authority, interest, and cause. There is a responsibility both of the giver and receiver of *kuleana*. We *malama* (take care of) the ocean and it provides us with food, transportation, and cleansing.

Make

Dead, death.

Malasada

A malasada is a Portuguese fried dough. It is a fried dough of flattened rounds flavored with lemon zest and coated with granulated sugar and cinnamon.

Source: Rachel Lauden's THE FOOD OF PARADISE: EXPLORING HAWAII'S CULINARY HERITAGE (University of Hawaii Press, 1996)

Malo

Traditionally, a *tapa* loin cloth worn by Hawaiian men.

Mu'umu'u

A loose, long dress adapted from the styles of the early New England missionaries.

Naʻu
Hawaiian word for mine or belonging to me.

Night Marchers (Huakaʻi-po)
In Hawaiian mythology, Night Marchers are the spirits of ancient Hawaiian warriors who guard the royals. Typically, when they are pictured, they are dressed for battle, wearing *malo* and gourd helmets, carrying long spears and clubs edged with shark teeth.

Night Marchers travel in a group. Signs of them coming are a foul, musky "death-like" rotten odor, torches, ground rumbling.

Ancient Hawaiians believed anyone looking at a Marcher will die. People should lie motionless, face down on the ground, to show proper respect and deference to be spared. If a Marcher recognizes a person, he may call "Naʻu!" which means "mine" in Hawaiian, and no one in the warrior procession will harm them.

Source: Martha Beckwith, HAWAIIAN MYTHOLGY. (University of Hawaii Press, 1970)

ʻOhana
ʻOhana means family, relative, kin. But as a cultural value it is central to Hawaiian culture. It is a foundation belief that one gives unconditional support, encouragement, understanding, and love to family. ʻOhana is extended to those who are not related by blood.

Paniolo
This is the Hawaiian word for cowboy that was based on the English word Spaniard. The cowboy tradition on the Big Island has a rich and long history.

Pio
There are several definitions for the Hawaiian word *pio*. Among

them are captured, prisoner, victim, prey, disappeared, gone out of sight.

Poha

The common name for *poha* berries is gooseberries. It is a fuzzy berry that makes a sweet and sour jam that is popular on the Big Island.

Source: University of Hawaii, College of Tropical Agriculture: https://gms.ctahr.hawaii.edu/gs/handler/getmedia.ashx-?moid=3096&dt=3&g=12

Puka

Puka means a hole in Hawaiian.

Pono

The translation of *pono* is goodness, morality, correct or proper, righteous, but its meaning goes beyond that. It is a way of life that is just, balanced, and in line with those values.
Completely proper. Right. Done well. In accordance with tradition and morals.

ABOUT ATMOSPHERE PRESS

Founded in 2015, Atmosphere Press was built on the principles of Honesty, Transparency, Professionalism, Kindness, and Making Your Book Awesome. As an ethical and author-friendly hybrid press, we stay true to that founding mission today.

If you're a reader, enter our giveaway for a free book here:

SCAN TO ENTER
BOOK GIVEAWAY

If you're a writer, submit your manuscript for consideration here:

SCAN TO SUBMIT
MANUSCRIPT

And always feel free to visit Atmosphere Press and our authors online at atmospherepress.com. See you there soon!

ABOUT THE AUTHOR

DOROTHEA N. BUCKINGHAM is an award-winning author, librarian, and certified book coach specializing in coaching historical fiction and memoir writing. Her previous books include: *My Name is Loa*, a middle-grade book about a young boy sent to the Molokai Leprosy Settlement in 1898; *Staring Down the Dragon*, an American Library Association Best Book for Young Adult Selection about a teenage girl returning to high school after having been treated for cancer; *Who Murdered Jane Stanford?*, an adult historical mystery based on the unsolved mystery of how Jane Stanford, wife of Senator Leland Stanford, died in Waikiki in 1905; and *Delicious Tidbits*, a historical review with recipes of Sackets Harbor, New York.

Dorothea lives in Kaneohe, Hawaii, with her husband and their ragamuffin dog, Rosie.

She can be reached directly at her website: DorotheaBuckingham. com. Dorothea also offers free posts about civilian life during World War 2 in Hawaii at https://dorotheanbuckingham.substack. com every Tuesday.